S

Maggie; or,
A Man and a Woman
Walk Into a Bar

Katie Yee

Summit Books

NEW YORK   AMSTERDAM/ANTWERP   LONDON
TORONTO   SYDNEY/MELBOURNE   NEW DELHI

Summit
Books

An Imprint of Simon & Schuster, LLC
1230 Avenue of the Americas
New York, NY 10020

For more than 100 years, Simon & Schuster has championed authors and the stories they create. By respecting the copyright of an author's intellectual property, you enable Simon & Schuster and the author to continue publishing exceptional books for years to come. We thank you for supporting the author's copyright by purchasing an authorized edition of this book.

This book is a work of fiction. Any references to historical events, real people, or real places are used fictitiously. Other names, characters, places, and events are products of the author's imagination, and any resemblance to actual events or places or persons, living or dead, is entirely coincidental.

First Summit Books hardcover edition July 2025

SUMMIT BOOKS and colophon are trademarks of Simon & Schuster, LLC

Simon & Schuster strongly believes in freedom of expression and stands against censorship in all its forms. For more information, visit BooksBelong.com.

For information about special discounts for bulk purchases, please contact Simon & Schuster Special Sales at 1-866-506-1949 or business@simonandschuster.com.

The Simon & Schuster Speakers Bureau can bring authors to your live event. For more information or to book an event, contact the Simon & Schuster Speakers Bureau at 1-866-248-3049 or visit our website at www.simonspeakers.com.

Interior design by Paul Dippolito

Manufactured in the United States of America

1   3   5   7   9   10   8   6   4   2

Library of Congress Cataloging-in-Publication Data is available on file.

ISBN 978-1-6680-8421-2
ISBN 978-1-6680-8423-6 (ebook)

For my family. Thanks for not laughing at me when I said I was going to study English.

Especially for my mom, from whom I inherited a love of stories.

I was folding linens when I first found out my children don't think I'm funny. I was by the hall closet, overhearing them asking my husband for a bedtime story. This was after I'd already read them *Where the Wild Things Are*, a book they used to love so much the pages were starting to pull from their binding. He reminded them of this. A good husband. And they told him, "You'd tell it better." And so he did. A better father.

The thing I noticed that was peculiar about my husband's telling was that the characters are all out of sorts. Max doesn't sail away from his room in the usual boat. A bald boy named Harold shows up, paddling past in an ill-drawn dinghy, clutching a purple crayon. As my husband tells it, they sail off together but lose their way. They float for what feels like days, until they happen upon an island they come to know as Neverland, where a ragtag gang of boys their age pulls them in. They were Lost Boys all along. Go figure.

It became a bad habit. I'd read them their story, kiss their sweaty foreheads, try not to step on Lincoln Logs on the way out. I'd tread downstairs, begin to soak the pots and pans, and then I'd stand in the hall, at the bottom of the staircase, listening to them beg my husband for a better story. It was a small betrayal. Night after night, he'd pluck a character from one book and drop it into another. The mismatched-ness made them laugh. It's unexpected; it's not right. That's what makes it fun. Little Red Riding Hood turning up at her

1

grandmother's house only to find, not Grandma, not the Wolf, no, but Sleeping Beauty instead.

And my kids are in fits over it.

It hurts in an unexpected way, like doing yoga for the first time in a long while and realizing you can't bend the way you thought you could; a new soreness.

*

We knew our children would look more like me, by the basic rules of genetics. In the world of procreation and Punnett squares, our bodies were not on equal footing. I possess the dominant traits: black hair, brown eyes, skin with warm undertones. For weeks of the babies' development, I imagined my genes looming large over his in the egg, devouring them. Something in it felt greedy. Also, powerful.

Sam has brown-blond hair, green eyes, and skin that loosely resembles pale shrimp gaining pink over the stove. He's tall, a whole head taller than me, with an effortlessly trim frame. It did make me sad to think of these traits, lost. The things that drew me to him initially.

After one doctor's appointment, after my husband went to bed, I studied my face in the mirror. Really studied. A widow's peak at the hairline, faint eyebrows, a nonexistent nose bridge, sparse eyelashes—the hair perhaps relocated to my knuckles, which I stacked rings on top of, every morning.

Other things that are inherited: a hitchhiker's thumb, the ability to touch tongue to nose, the willingness of your fingers to split into the "live long and prosper" signal.

I have on good authority (an OB nurse holding court at a friend's holiday party) that when they are born, children most resemble the father. They have evolved to do so, so the dad will recognize himself in his offspring—and not think them the product of a torrid affair. Even the evolution of newborns assumes a world rife with infidelity. Even babies know to appease the patriarch, to make it known that they are his.

*

I'm at the bookstore with my best friend, Darlene. She's picking up Jeanette Winterson's *Written on the Body* to impress someone she likes. I think of early days, of the effort you make just to show someone you're interested.

By the register, there are all these little tchotchke gifts for people you don't know well. The desk calendars shine with their plastic, and their promise of twelve inoffensive whales, or national parks, or what have you. There are also books on a spinning rack: *The Little Book of Buddhism, Love Poems, Fun Facts About Birds,* and *A Beginner's Guide to Paris.* Then there it is: *The Big Book of Anti-Jokes.*

Darlene thinks I'm being dramatic when I tell her about the kids not finding me funny anymore. It's usually her job to talk me down from these things, to stop my little spirals. "They used to find me hilarious," I protest to her. I try to balance *The Big Book of Anti-Jokes* on my head. "Remember *Is This a Hat?* They loved that one." (Darlene hated that one, how many hours spent asking the same question.) Let me tell you something: children are tickled by wrongness. Or maybe they just love knowing something you don't.

I tell her the anti-joke book is for me, not them, and it turns into an anti-lie. I keep it, and then I just keep keeping it. The jokes are like flat soda. The punch lines are more like weak kicks in areas

3

you don't expect, that don't even hurt. The jokes make no sense. Rather, they make a little too much sense. The anti-jokes pare all the theatrics of jokes down to naked logic. (What do you call a joke that isn't funny? A sentence. Want to hear something that'll make you smile? Your face muscles.) I find myself reading them after everyone else has turned in for the night. Sometimes, I think to text one or two to Darlene, or even to my husband upstairs, but I don't think they'll truly appreciate them. I rifle through the pages quiet as I can and feel like a kid unwrapping candy, sneaking just one or two more in before bed.

*

Sometimes I dream of being a children's book author. I can picture my byline on the glossy cover. All the kids will put their sticky hands on my name but never say it out loud. (This is okay. I find comfort in this, actually: a near-anonymous dependability.)

I would write down all the stories that used to delight my kids— some of which we made up together. They might not love hearing them forever, but I could store them in the pages of my children's book for safekeeping. I would write down all the stories I dream up that I'm too afraid to tell them. (Your most cutting critics are always your children.)

I would write from the perspective of Darlene's dog, Roberta, who believes, whenever it rains, that her human has mistakenly opened up the wrong door into another reality; I would write about a peculiar store that sells sleep by the inch, happiness by the pound, wisdom in spools, and love in degrees; I would write about Harold the Elephant, whose job it is to sit in uncomfortable silence among humans whenever something isn't being said, whose job it was to be the literal elephant in the room. Then Harold would go home to his elephant family, from whom he was keeping a secret of his own, and there would be a human in the room.

I read a rather demoralizing study that said that in one year, they surveyed all the children's books published in the US. Here's what they found: Roughly half the books published centered white characters. Also: more books were published starring animals or inanimate objects than all the books about people of color combined.

"So, fix it! Write this down!" Darlene, indignant, says when I tell her this. Her excitement fuels me, and I sit down to write and—nothing.

Truthfully, I'm not sure how to tell people my stories yet. The characters in my own family are starting to feel so opaque to me; it seems like an awful lot of effort to create new life and to get to know them, too. Besides, I'm reluctant to pluck my own flesh and blood and place them there, in my stories. I don't want to spin them into something against their will. I want them to live fully off the page, no shadow wet with my ink following them around.

*

There was a loud baby on my first date with my husband. At a trendy Asian fusion restaurant, in the booth behind ours. I said something about myself, and the baby cried. "Baby doesn't like that," he joked, and the baby behind us became a barometer for how well things were going.

Sam chose this restaurant because it was very vegetarian-friendly. "Not because I'm Asian," I had clarified, teasing him. "Of course not," he'd said. I was adamantly vegetarian in those days. Sam even converted for the first several years of our dating life and subsequent marriage, falling into the soft pillow of my habits. On our wedding day, he couldn't resist the siren sound of "Chicken or beef?" and caved once, and okay, sometimes on special occasions. ("Bacon doesn't count on birthdays, right?") But the years since have turned him back into a carnivore, someone who devours the flesh of weaker animals.

*

When you first start dating someone, early communication is communal. Everybody knows that. When you're texting a woman, it's incredibly probable that you're talking not just to her but to one or two of her closest friends as well. You need a group consensus.

When we first started dating, eventually Sam caught on to this and sent a message that went something like, "Hello, ladies." Ladies? "Ladies?" I had replied. "Yeah, since you're going to show this to Darlene anyway," he joked.

At the wedding, Darlene joked that she had courtship-side seats.

*

At night, I can hear my husband spinning new stories for the kids, really selling them on it. The Tortoise and the Hare are in a race, but it's the Big Bad Wolf who wins in the end.

The children protest. How can this be? They demand to know. "I thought slow and steady won the race," my son, the skeptic, says. I hear the creak of bedsprings, my husband shifting his weight.

There's a small reading lamp on the nightstand between their twin beds. It's like a gold orb with lots of tiny dots poked into it, from which the light shines out. From my perch in the hallway, with their door open, I can see their blurry shadows. I learn to tell the difference: my daughter, Lily, trying hard not to fall asleep, the gentle sway of slumber cast over her; Noah, my son, leaning intently forward, toward the story. My husband's shadow looms so large over theirs. Some evenings, if they're slumped close together, his shadow completely consumes theirs, and it's like they are one cohesive thing.

My voyeuristic obsession reminds me of the allegory of the cave. Prisoners facing a wall, doomed to watch the puppet show of life play out in front of them. How different reality is from here. How stubborn we are not to see what's lurking, right behind us.

My husband clears his throat and tells them, "Can't you see? It's really a good thing he won the race that day. It means he wasn't there to huff and puff and blow those nice pigs' house down."

*

A man and a woman walk into a bar. It sounds like the start of a very old joke, and it is. It is also the start of an affair.

*

When my husband told me about Maggie, we were out, kidless, at a nice Indian restaurant. I should have known something was up. But the restaurant we were at was actually an all-you-can-eat buffet, so one can imagine the excitement that blinded me.

The plates they give you at those things are never as large as you want them to be. They trust that you will not want to get up and down and pace around the buffet table so much, but I requested we get the table right in front of it. "So we'll see when they replenish the samosas," I said to my husband, who simply shook his head but sat down across from me, the way he always had.

He laid the red linen napkin across his lap, which reminded me to do the same. My husband, always the man with good manners. (When we first moved in together, with no furniture to speak of, we sat on the hardwood floor and ordered Papa John's. I remember he laid a tiny paper napkin across his knee with a great flourish that night, and I remember remembering that moment at the restaurant. Funny, isn't it? The things that stick.)

The first part of the evening was marvelous. An all-you-can-eat buffet! A place of possibility. I gorged on garlic naan and saag paneer. We drank creamy mango lassis out of stout goblets.

Having the table near the buffet meant we got a lot of foot traffic. This, of course, made it incredibly awkward when my husband finally said what it was that he wanted to say. I remember thinking he had been eyeing the buffet line with a rare intensity all evening. At first, I thought he was just eager to get his second fill when the line was shortest. In hindsight, I think he was timing it such that no one would be within earshot when he said it.

I had been in a good mood that day, on account of the surprise fancy dinner. ("Don't get too excited. It's really not *that* nice," Sam had said when I was opening the door and making little exclamations of joy. When I was growing up, my family didn't eat out at restaurants much, and there are some things you never grow out of.) I was yammering on about some gossip from the PTA, a very minor treasury scandal that isn't worth dwelling on. Then I guess my husband saw his moment—a clearing of the cars, a log to float on—and said it. Four little words. "I'm having an affair."

Honestly, my first inclination was to laugh. Not because what he said was funny at all, no, but because his confession was just so surprising. It's been my experience that when you're confronted with something you don't know what to do with, the human body sort of just naturally, nervously, guffaws. I thought, surely it was part of a joke I wasn't quite getting. One of Sam's bits. Sometimes he says totally random things just to see if people are listening, like a mic check. He just wants a reaction out of you. Like the mix-and-match game he played with the kids at bedtime, only with higher stakes. Risky. A bad punch line. *I'm having an affair.* Just like that. A punch to the gut.

I watched his face for signs of a joke: the curl of a smile tugging at his lips, but his mouth stayed in that same sharp line. Could a mouth be so piercing?

It was the floor giving out. The Wolf after all. (When I would tell this story over and over again to Darlene—a way to process—we would take to calling it "a total naan-sequitur.")

In romance movies, when you meet the person you're supposed to be with, time parts. It has a way of happening around the two lovers. In action films, when someone dies, there is that similar slowing down. Time bends for those on the precipice.

Anyway, *I'm having an affair.* Sam's words hung solidly in the air. They didn't dissipate like some phrases ("love you" after the "I" has been dropped). That night, time stretched to accommodate my delay in response.

The natural first question: Who is she? They say that the human brain is incapable of creating faces. This means that every stranger you encounter in a dream is, in fact, someone who exists in real life. In this waking nightmare, it was the same. It was someone I knew, surely. Someone I had seen, even in passing: a perky assistant at work; one of his more serious ex-girlfriends crawling out of the woodwork after all this time; a woman in a beige raincoat waiting for the bus; a very fit runner with a sleek ponytail jogging next to him in the early morning; our favorite barista, who hands us our large drip coffees every morning but only charges us for smalls.

Prolonged eye contact; beating around the bush; the electricity of a carefully planned casual touch to the arm; sharing a HuffPost article because it reminded you; a totally innocent and coincidental run-in at a coffee shop on the other side of town; splitting a pastry; the way the possibility of a missed text message can burn a hole in your pocket; the siren glow of a phone screen in the middle of the night; "I was just thinking about you"; the intensity of a long-delayed first kiss; teasing photos; dinner at her place, cold plates, candles, sinking into the couch like a slow and willful slide into the mud; deleted text messages (on his end—whoever she is, I'm sure she's kept it all).

In the wickedness of my imagination, even in that split second, from the depths of my subconscious, I pictured her as a white woman. Pretty. Dirty blond. They could be siblings. That type of thing. Even in that blink of a moment, I somehow knew. Conjured up this person who looked like she fit a little better next to Sam.

I replayed all our interactions of the past few months. Counted the number of nights he was late coming in from the office—the way I pitied him and said he should stop working so hard, heated his dinner and hung up his coat, the pockets of which were probably still warm from some other woman's touch. Counted the number of times I woke up with his back to me, his phone screen obscured, and I had assumed it was merely another news alert from the *New York Times* informing us of bombs dropping somewhere else.

They weren't so much concrete thoughts or fully formed sentences as they were quick emotions and scenarios I was moving through. I almost have to hand it to my imagination for the speed with which it could create a dozen vignettes: images (lives, love stories) flickering through my mind like the flame from the tea candle on the table.

And then the second wave hit me, and I felt guilty about my own reaction. His admission made me feel like we were in the earlier days of our dating life somehow. Brought forth *wife* and *partner* instead of *mother*. The family fell away for just a second. We weren't one unit any longer. Something about his having an affair made it between me and him in a way things hadn't been for a while. For just a second, in this conversation, the years shrank down and the betrayal was to some younger version of myself: a girl on a first date, a girl at her wedding, a girl with a broken heart. Deer—headlights.

Not wanting to look at him, I kept my eyes trained on the buffet table instead. A man was emptying an entire tray of samosas onto the platter. The steam that rose out of them smelled heavenly.

I'm having an affair—like it's something you possess and not something you've done. Like, *I'm having highlights done next week.* Like, *I'm having lamb over rice.*

"I'm having seconds," I said, and abruptly stood up, my napkin falling to the floor. I piled the samosas up high on my plate. I ate them all, and we didn't say anything more. The whole rest of that meal, I remember, Sam kept his gaze firmly fixed on me. You could've warmed my plate with the heat of his stare.

It reminded me of that advice about being robbed or held up at gunpoint. You're supposed to make as much eye contact with your villain as possible, to solidify your humanness. It was like Sam was trying to telepath to me some proof of his humanity.

A man and a different woman walk into a restaurant, and it sounds like the start of a very old joke, and it is. It is also the end of a marriage.

*

My husband has no obsessions. He's not a hobbyist or a tinkerer. He doesn't dabble. We tried roller-skating on an early date and left after he fell down once; he gives the impression of a man in control of his time because he doesn't bother with things he's not good at. He doesn't like working toward something. It's in these ways you can tell he was the golden boy growing up. The smooth finish of an easy life. A life without turbulence.

He became a headhunter because he's good at talking people into things, selling them on some other way their life could be. If this were one of his fairy tales, my husband would be a mysterious merchant, a stranger blowing through town on the wind. He would have a small burlap satchel that he would never let go of. He would arrive in a place and go door-to-door and sell mortals another life that could be theirs. His powers would hinge on the irresistibility of snow not trodden on—all the paths you've never walked down. And if you don't read the fine print, he'll make off with your children.

My children, of course, find my husband's job funny. They tell their friends in hushed tones that their father is a "head hunter" when they come over, as they are removing their sneakers by the front door. If their friends sleep over that night, I notice they pull the sheets up a little higher around their cheeks, like a shield. The kids think it's fun to lord their dad's perceived power over people like this.

What my husband being a headhunter actually means, of course, is that he is always looking for the best person for the job. He knows what to offer to get someone's attention. And he has to sacrifice very little in the end. The choices don't affect his day-to-day living very much.

*

Once, in my early twenties, I got this little compact mirror that I kept in my purse. I loved it—carried it with me everywhere—but I didn't use it very often. One day, it shattered, only I didn't realize it. For weeks, I would stick my hand in my bag and come up cut and not know why. When I think of the night Sam told me about Maggie, it feels like that.

Everyone says bad things happen in a blur, but I remember the rest of that evening sharply.

At the all-you-can-eat restaurant: I finished my second plate. Sam pushed cubes of paneer around with his fork, trying to catch my eye. I can still hear the specific and grating scrape of his fork on those sturdy off-white plates. When the check came, Sam signed it. Then out came two tiny scoops of mango rice pudding. My husband removed the spoon that was supposed to be his from the rim, and gestured for me to take the whole thing, which I did; it was delicious, the best rice pudding I've had to this day. How do you like that?

On the way home: the train was delayed. Fourteen minutes away, according to the announcements board, which might as well have said an eternity. "Do you want to just take a cab?" my husband asked, somewhere just behind me and to the left. I shook my head, resigned to the underground, to the waiting. *What am I rushing toward anyway?* There was a young couple—high school—making out on the platform. They had an impressive height difference between them, and backpacks. They did not look popular, which made me hope they were happy. *Don't spend it all in one place,* I telepathed to them. Seventeen minutes later, a rat ran valiantly over a medium-sized UA Theater soda cup in the tracks, just before our chariot arrived, and I found myself rooting for it. Wanting to root for life.

The train: was empty enough that we could sit together but didn't have to. We did anyway, in one of those love seats by the window, cramped. It reminded me of the first date, how under the table, you might lean a knee daringly toward the other person. We both winced when the train's turbulence pushed us toward one another. Sam put his feet up on the seat in front of us, and I noticed for the first time the way they maybe didn't quite fit; the way the edges of his leather shoes were worn thin and light from the friction of his step.

Every few stops, my curiosity got the better of me, and I broke my pseudo-silent treatment. I asked the requisite questions: who, what, when, etc. *Who* first because I needed another villain, one I wasn't married to. Who is she? How did you meet? (How did this happen?) And then the train would rumble over the tracks. The closer we got to home, the harder the questions got. But I held on to *why.* I thought I knew the answer to this one: he had simply met someone better. In truth, I think I had always felt a tad inferior to Sam. The lack of my *why* made this clear. Besides, the other questions were more fact-based, whereas *why* tiptoed into an emotional realm I wasn't quite ready for. It required more personal excavation. I could be roped into the *why.* The interrogation lamp would turn to shine on our marriage and its failures in his eyes. I didn't want to see what came to light. Instead, I asked: Have you slept with her? (Is she better in bed?) Do you love her? (Do you love her more than you love me?)

A resolute "yes" to the questions I asked answered the questions I didn't.

Approaching the front door: I got my keys out first. Like so many women, I'm used to walking with them in between my fingers at night. I fumbled with the lock because it sticks at inconvenient times, and then I let us both in, and it is not a metaphor for anything. It's not a metaphor, not a blur, I remember it all so crystal clear.

Like a superhero or a big cat with good reflexes, I swear my senses were heightened that evening. I remember every detail in an attempt to—what?

We got home, and home felt different. Smaller. Like somebody who is very good with pranks got a contractor to shrink every room by eleven inches, give or take. Like maybe the prankster and the contractor put up a second wall, see, so everything comes in just a touch closer.

Coming home was like being jolted from a dream, jarred into a small and insignificant life. Tinged with embarrassment, too. That shine I thought my life had? Fool's gold after all. The way you can tell the difference: when pressure is applied to the surface, real gold will indent (receptive to impression, to being sculpted), whereas fool's gold will merely flake and crumble.

Barring that, everything was exactly as I had left it, and that somehow made everything worse. The seltzer can I had placed on the kitchen counter on my way out with three or four little sips inside—I drank from it, suddenly parched, when we returned, the bubbles flat. The fizz out of life.

Like coming back from a glamorous vacation and having the jolting realization that—surprise!—you live in filth. The piles of kids' laundry hiding behind doors. The minuscule splatters on the stove that you always mean to get out but never do. The way enough stray hairs find each other in the corners of rooms and accumulate their own personhood.

I noticed our mess with the eyes of a stranger, of someone coming into our home for the first time. I looked at our home the way she might have seen it. I saw the streaks on the windows and the overflowing kitchen trash can, the balled-up fleece blankets on the couch. Shoes at the entryway, kicked this way and that. I saw all the little lived-in flaws, the way you might be passingly critical of these things in someone else's home, or a hotel room. When you see a few stray hairs in the bathroom sink of an Airbnb, you think that's disgusting, but when they're from your own head, you think nothing of it. Maybe that's what it is. Every stray hair now felt like an encroachment.

Had she been here at all? Maybe when I was shuffling the kids to birthday parties and making small talk with the other parents, comparing notes on the new second-grade teacher over ice cream cake? Maybe when I was taking the kids for checkups, which we tried to stack onto one day a year: Pit Crew Day? Perhaps when we were going to the movies with Darlene, but Sam had to back out at the last second for some transatlantic call that his assistant messed up the time zones for?

Had she seen the house in this state and loved him still? Did she take one look around and judge my housekeeping? Did she say to herself: *No wonder why. She can't even keep her own home in order?* Did she think, maybe, just to make herself feel better, that the state of our home was a reflection on the state of our marriage? I hadn't thought it was so dire. Maybe just a tad neglected. Sure, the recycling was overflowing and there were garbage bags of outgrown clothes to be donated in the front hallway, but our intentions were so good!

All the grime stuck with me and I did not bother washing it off. I wanted to remember it all. About this, I wonder: Why?

To keep this story from tumbling away from me, maybe, out of control, out of my grasp. I dug the talons of my memory deep into that night, and I didn't let go for a very long time.

The kids' sneakers and socks kicked off exactly where they stood when they got home; the throw pillow basically still holding Noah's shape from where he fell asleep on the couch earlier that afternoon. I looked around at our family mess, with less criticism and with more love. Already longing for the way we lived like this.

*

The night he tells me about Maggie is the first night when I dream of being alone in my house. It's a dream I will have over and over with no variation, but this night, I'm sure, is the first time I dream it. It's dark. There's a *knock-knock* at the door. ("Definitely the result of too many of those jokes before bed," Darlene chastises me when I tell the story later.)

In the dream, I'm in the middle of something, and I can never remember what it is by the time I wake up. All I know is that I'm reluctant to get the door. I think of the things that typically come knocking: opportunity, or death. Witches with baskets of apples. Mean wolves with hardy lungs.

"Who's there?" I ask, in every dream. The question, a line of defense. The joke relies on the natural human instinct to want to know who is on the other side of the door. Your identity becomes the password that way.

When I finally turn the knob and swing back the door, there is no one there.

*

By the time I wake up the next morning, Sam is already dressed for work. He's wearing a very handsome navy-blue suit, one I picked out with him years ago to celebrate a promotion at work. It's early—not even six a.m. He spent the night on the couch. It wasn't something we discussed; he just surrendered himself to it like a martyr. When we got to the house, he simply said, "I'll give you some time to process," and dismissed himself. It was late. I didn't have it in me to pick a fight anyway. When I wake, it's to the sound of his weekender duffel bag being zipped up. Such a final sound.

"I think I'm going to stay at my parents' house for a while," he ventures quietly. "And then we can sort everything out."

Sam's parents live in this enormous house in Oyster Bay, about an hour's drive away. Well, *live* is maybe not the right word. They own several properties, this house among them. His family is the kind of generous that means always letting people stay in their houses, but only when they aren't around. This was maybe the first time I looked at Sam and saw empty houses, too.

Whenever we would stay in this version of their home, we would drive up and all the blinds would be shut. The lights off. The heat off. Severe. Because Sam's parents liked to bounce around a lot, they didn't bother with plants. Their homes were devoid of life in every way.

When we first started driving up there on a few odd weekends of the year, the kids were initially afraid of the house. We'd usually depart on a Friday, whenever Sam could get away from work, which is to say it was usually dark—the sun having slipped away, abandoning us before our arrival. We'd park the car, and Noah would just start wailing, which made Lily cry, too. The four of us, sitting in our little Subaru, with this big, intimidating house before us. "It's haunted!" Noah would cry and cry. He hated opening doors. He refused to pull back the shower curtain in the bathroom by himself, unsure of what he might find. Lily feared the dark space under her bed, conjured up all sorts of evils that might make their home there. Don't even get them started on the stairs to the basement and the ladder to the attic!

But one day, to ward off the ghosts and whatever else had settled there, I came up with this silly ritual for us. I would arm the children with their own little camping lanterns. This part was important, that the lanterns belonged to them. They got to choose the ones they wanted. My kids would go forward with unborrowed light. I would put on Toploader's "Dancing in the Moonlight." Really blast it from the car speakers. I feel it is scientifically impossible to be upset or mad or afraid when this song is playing. (Also, it was Sam's and my wedding song. Something we played often in our own home, and that familiarity gave them added comfort.)

We made a game of it. They would run through the house with this song blasting, and they would flip every switch they could find.

Sam and I would stand outside on the porch and watch the warmth spread room by room, as if by magic. We would watch our kids flood the space with light and life. And by the time the song was over, all the lights would be on, and the kids and Sam and I would be singing the last of the lyrics in the foyer under the crystal chandelier, awash in its glow. Whispering the last of the song as it faded out into the normalcy of the rest of our night.

And now it seemed incredibly likely that we wouldn't be doing that again, ever.

Instead: Sam would drive up to that big, imposing house alone. Would our song play somewhere in the back of his mind? Or, no— would he be there with her? Tonight, would they pull up together with some totally different and new song on the radio? Would they have spent the drive dreaming about their future together and meaning it this time? That's the way it is with new love: pulling your dreams from the clouds and laying them out before you like brickwork. Assuming they'll be solid enough to hold you. Isn't it funny—when we think of dreams, we think ethereal. Lofty. Gauzy even. And it's true: when it was me and Sam in that car at the very beginning, my wants were all so airy and unspecific. I wanted to be loved. I wanted a nice life. And I wanted it with Sam, plain and simple. Would he lead her into the guest bedroom where we always stayed? (Maybe I always felt like a guest in that house. Maybe his family always saw me as a transient person, a way station for their Sam.) My dreams are so heavy now. When did that happen? Maybe it's something that comes with age. Or family.

Our house is already starting to feel like Sam's parents' house on the beach when you approach it at night. When I hear Sam shut the front door and drive away, I close my eyes, and I understand better what Noah and Lily were feeling when they looked into the soulless house that was not a home. You're never too old to be afraid of what you can't see. How scary it is to be in the dark of things.

*

Darlene and I are separated by a thirty-two-minute walk that encompasses part of our local park: a few miles of greenery to make you forget you live in a congested metropolis. I come to the park to participate in the shared delusion of calm, of life somewhere else, and sometimes it works! After muttering a meek explanation about their father's sudden "business-related" departure and walking them to school, I embark on my tiny odyssey and pray for a poetic rain. Something to make everyone miserable with me, or at the very least to keep my few escaped tears company. It's a beautiful spring day. How wildly disjointed it is when the sun on your skin feels like it's mocking you.

I tell Darlene that I need to come over but not why. It feels like the kind of news best delivered in person. Still, I dial her number as I weave my way through late-morning commuters and semipro cyclists.

Even over the phone, I can feel everything in her trying not to ask me what is going on. We dance around the proverbial elephant. I ask about her life: attentive questions regarding her dog's progress on "paw" and "other paw." (No progress to speak of; thank you for asking.) I ask about updates on that one new coworker she has been having problems with (still an asshole) and about how her date went the other night (an asshole, as of recently). It's not like I don't want to check in. I just know that once I get to her, I'll need the full floor.

Darlene and I had the good fortune of being matched up as

college roommates. We joked that it was kind of racist that they paired us together, being two of the few non-white people on our liberal arts campus. We had nothing in common, aside from maybe a baseline of understanding born from our shared exclusion.

When we first met, Darlene was hanging up a poster of *The Silence of the Lambs* in our dorm room. She binged horror movies and wore her love of them like a badge of honor; I couldn't even sit through the previews for them in theaters. She tolerated men; I chased them with abandon. I read books; she read music. She smoked cigarettes, drank vodka without mixers, gave me antacid before nights out so I wouldn't turn red after one drink, and taught me how to dance one night by telling me to write my name in the air with my hips. I once walked in on her getting a stick-and-poke tattoo from our RA. Me? I only drank Mike's Hard Lemonade at the time, and the truth is I'd never done a risky thing in my life before we met. I went to college to learn how to write. Without Darlene, my path through those four years would've been a straight and easily traceable line: from my bed to the library and back. I could've lived my life like a hologram.

My mom drilled into me at a young age that success meant not being valued for manual labor. She worked at a garment factory, sewing on the line in Chinatown. She hated it. She didn't want me anywhere near it, but she was good at it: following patterns, putting things together. Sometimes she'd take fabric home with her; when she was sure no one was looking, she would slide a few pieces into her purse at the end of the shift: black velvet with purple roses; red linen; a silky electric blue. She never thought much of her own creations—they were patchwork, practical, something for me to cloak my body with. But to me, putting on something my mother had crafted was like being enshrined. Those were my best days. Yes, my mother was always good at taking the scraps of life and turning them into something worthwhile.

When I was growing up, I was not told that I was pretty. Nor was I ever complimented for being kind or sweet or helpful, for playing well with others. My teachers would say these nice things during parent-teacher conferences, and I would dutifully translate, only to have my parents shake their heads and ask instead how my grades compared to everyone else's. If I won a little gold medal during a field day activity at school, I was not fawned over for being fast. Quick wit was the only speed that mattered in my house.

Before school, my mom would wake me up early so she could brush and braid my hair. This was less about maintaining appearances and more about ensuring that her child would focus on the lesson plan instead of futzing with her hair. Back then, it grew so fast, was so long that I could nearly sit on it. It also got knots, constantly, which took a long time to comb out, but I didn't mind because it meant more time as the sole object of my mother's trained attention. She'd put on her drugstore reading glasses—dark red, a color she was particularly fond of and excited to have found in frames—which always made me feel a little bit like a story she was in the middle of.

I would only be noticed for my intelligence, taught that climbing up in this world wasn't supposed to resemble a physical trial. In this way, I learned to live outside my body.

But Darlene, a visual artist, lived her life with a tangibility I had never imagined wanting. She made indentations in mounds of clay until they resembled something. She was not afraid to splatter paint. She lived her life with a drop cloth handy. She moved through the world in big, bold strokes.

We had absolutely nothing in common, but we met at that perfect malleable age; we shaped each other.

In those college days, we would do this weird thing where, if one of us needed to vent, that person would quite literally lie on the floor in the center of our shared room. The venter starfishes out, speaks their peace—uninterrupted—and without the margin of judgment cast by inadvertent facial expressions of the other party. It's calming. Metaphorically, it satisfies something about being at your lowest point with the solidness of the ground beneath you.

When Darlene opens her apartment door, I see she's already cleared the space for me.

As I detail for Darlene what happened, I find myself fixating on this one spot where the wall hits the molding before it becomes ceiling. We painted one wall of her apartment a deep shade of eggplant a few years ago, when accent walls were all the rage. ("I never get my security deposits back anyway," she had said, when we were picking out shades of purple in Home Depot.) We rented a ladder and bought paint rollers and honestly did a pretty great job, except for this one spot on the ceiling where a fleck of purple had made its home against the white. I look at the spot and it feels like that spot was my life somehow. The stain we brought on.

"What the fuck," Darlene says when I'm finished. Somewhere in the kitchen, her teakettle starts whistling. "Sorry, let me get that," she says, but when she returns, it's with two Bloody Marys instead. "I'm out of celery," she apologizes, and we clink glasses even though there is nothing to celebrate.

Of course we stalk her on the internet immediately. We have only her first name, and the fact that Sam met her through work, to go on, but that proves to be enough. Darlene finds her on

LinkedIn in a matter of seconds. "Shit," she says, staring at the screen. "She's cute."

In Maggie's LinkedIn profile picture, she is wearing a generic black blazer with a matching turtleneck underneath. In those two inches, her outfit makes her look like she is impersonating Elizabeth Holmes impersonating Steve Jobs. She is undeniably, as Darlene said, cute. She has green eyes and long, wavy brown hair that she highlighted blond. She smiles with her teeth, which are almost perfectly straight except for one in the bottom row, which makes her look more approachable somehow.

"White women," Darlene says, exasperated.

Of course it wasn't lost on me that Maggie was white. It added another layer to the betrayal. On the other hand, would it have been better if she were Chinese? Of course not. While choosing another Asian woman would have screamed fetish, the fact that it was a white woman begged the question of regret. Did he feel that in choosing me, he had chosen wrong?

Her page reveals that she changed jobs four months ago—in which case, they probably met at least a few weeks prior to that. I mine memory. What was going on then? Five or six months ago. They must have met sometime in the fall and fallen in love in the dreamy expanse of winter. The snow, a blank slate. Holiday shopping. Our son had two lines in the school play. Our daughter had an ear infection and wasn't sleeping well.

"Do you think he already loved her at Christmas?" I wonder. If he felt any guilt as he sat at the dinner table and cut into the Cornish game hen like nothing was the matter. If it pained him to accept the enthusiastic thanks of our kids for the presents I picked out and signed his name to. If he got her anything, too.

"I'm going to kill him! We could pull a real 'Goodbye Earl.' I mean it." She begins to pace. "I'm serious."

"I know you are," I say. "But don't. My kids still need their father." She groans. "Right, that." To Roberta, who is doing a little stretch-yawn on the couch, she says, "Don't get too attached to anyone I bring home, okay?"

*

That night, after the kids have been tucked in and read *Sylvester and the Magic Pebble*, I go into our bedroom and shut the door. I pull up Maggie's LinkedIn page again. Of course, I know there are better ways, better websites, to find out more about her, but there's time for that. For now, this is what I can handle. For now, I click on her profile picture. Presumably, this is the first photo my husband ever saw of her. I try to put myself in Sam's shoes. Try to see what he sees. Sure, she's pretty. Very pretty, actually. Everything is proportional. But what about her was *so* special? If you look carefully, you'll notice a cute little nose piercing, which I overlooked the first time. I study her face until I can conjure it when I close my eyes, like she's someone I know. When I eventually drift into sleep, I even see her in my dreams that night. She's just a floating head, and she doesn't say anything, just stares at me. And after I wake up, after I bring the kids to school and go about my day, I see her everywhere. For days, for weeks, sometimes even now—sometimes I'll turn a corner, and there she'll be, waiting for me.

"Look at where you live! Two new bougie coffee shops opened up on this block just last month, and you prioritized a 'good school district,'" Darlene says, when I confess this madness to her. "Look around!" We are indeed waiting for my kids to get out of school. An ice cream truck plays its siren sound somewhere behind us. Cliques

26

of parents are starting to gather for pickup, and I give Darlene a look that says she should lower her voice. Whispering, she says, "I could throw a rock and hit ten women who look just like her."

*

When you're a kid, you're so certain about the person you want to become. It's something they drill into you at a young age: name, age, grade, favorite color, what you want to be when you grow up. That simple. Of course, when you're a kid, there are also only like ten possible jobs: teacher, singer, professional baseball player, actor, ballerina, astronaut, president of the United States, doctor, fire-fighter, marine biologist. Plus, maybe whatever your parents do, if they don't happen to do one of those ten things.

(When my son was in kindergarten, there was a girl in his class whose parents were both therapists, and she always wanted to talk about it. She explained the job as "someone who knows all the se-crets." The whole class was hooked. That whole year, they all wanted to be therapists.)

When I was Noah's age, I decided I wanted to be a writer. I had read Andrew Clements's *The School Story*—a book that taught me that kids were allowed to write stories, that they too had something to say. It gave me permission. (It also made promises about the ease of the path to publication.)

I clung to that identity. I thought it fit me in the way few other identities did at the time. I chased this sense of self through high school and to college. (Much to the dismay of my extended family: "Why would she study English? She already speaks English!")

Eventually, the dream caved under the weight of more tangible realities.

There's a video somewhere on the internet of a raccoon who has gotten his hands on a tuft of cotton candy. Off he goes to the river—he can't believe his luck! He begins to wash it, as is his routine, but the cotton candy disappears, slips right between his fingers without his comprehension. That's what my dreams feel like some days. I wake up and I can't quite say what happened to them. Wrenched from my hands; lost to the river.

In real adult life, I'm shocked when I hear about jobs that I never knew existed. I'll be at a friend's wedding, and someone will say they're a large-animal veterinarian, and I'll have nothing to say except, "*Really*, what's *that* like?" and bask in a life I never knew was an option.

At PTA meetings alone, we've got a woman whose sole job it is to pick out the art for rich people's houses and upscale dentists' offices; a Lego artist; and a man who does those neat chalk signs at Trader Joe's. ("Putting my art degree to good use," he joked. "No, that's actually *so* cool! I hear they're a great company to work for," everyone said encouragingly.) We've got a woman who used to be what they called a "dream maker" at a swanky hotel chain, whose job revolved around remembering the names and small details of high-profile clients and doing whatever she could to make the stay as "personal" as possible (like having champagne automatically sent over to an old couple's table because it was their thirty-fifth wedding anniversary), and a professional name reader for hire at graduations (seasonal work).

Darlene does something with nonprofits and grants. Plus, ceramics on the side. I think that's the identity she'd prefer was cemented in people's impressions of her. She runs an Etsy shop, Urned It™, where she makes urns for the things we've loved and are ready to let go of. Urns for bad habits. Urns for people or relationships we're leaving in the past. (The idea came after her *last, last, last cigarette* senior year of college. Honestly, it was mostly just a really ornate and impractical ashtray until the final one for real. Then we put the lid on it.)

Darlene's urns are the opposite of funeral urns. They are not understated or subtle. They come in pastels and neons. They scream with life. Some of the pricier ones even have glitter and feathers. Celebration urns: sometimes the end is a good thing.

*

After he tells me about Maggie, I start to feel an ache in my chest. It's a dull ache to the touch, but solid as stone. Darlene says I'm manifesting my pain. If this were a different kind of story, the pain would give way to a Greek goddess daughter who would split open my breast and say something about feminism and who would just be mine. Or it would reveal itself to be a hole and my husband would get sucked up into it. Or it would need to be removed and it would confound doctors because it'd be a fig seed, and my husband and I would come back together to plant it, and then we'd get a tree. Sylvia Plath's fig tree of possible selves, and it would all be a big fat, juicy metaphor.

What really happened: a woman walks into an examination room. And it's cancer. There, that'll knock 'em dead.

*

Everything about my new ob-gyn has a soothing quality. She speaks in a low, lulling voice that rivals that of Delilah on 106.7 Lite FM. She's got long, dark, frizzy hair that cloaks her and makes her look

29

just disheveled enough that you feel like you can trust her. I don't like my doctors to be too polished. (It renders them untouchable, inhuman, so overtly better than me.)

Darlene is the one who recommended her after my last ob-gyn sold her practice. "You're going to love my doctor," Darlene promised. "She's a gentle soul. Very Mother Earth."

The sign on her door reads Dr. Leila Wei. Even her name is composed of soft, round sounds.

The nurse who leads me into the small exam room is so quiet. She is the opposite of a hairdresser. She says nothing reassuring. She gives me instructions about what to take off, what direction the robe should be facing, things like that. Then she closes the door, and I realize I have absolutely no memory of what she just said, on account of the conga line of worry running through my mind. Of course, the shirt and the bra need to be removed. That seems like a given. Underwear can probably stay on, but what about pants? I take off my socks for no real reason, and then I am cold and embarrassed and in the middle of putting my socks back on when the doctor knocks on the door and enters the room.

I let the other sock fall to the floor. If she notices, she doesn't say anything.

The art in Dr. Wei's exam room is all pastel-washed landscapes. I ask her about them, and she tells me that she paints them herself. "Sometimes with household objects," she tells me. "I made those stars by flicking white paint off a toothbrush."

"You're really good," I say, and mean it. "You didn't want to pursue art?"

"My parents wanted me to do something a little more practical." Understanding passes between us. "But I find that being a doctor and being an artist are very similar. You have to be good at pattern recognition—that's all diagnosis is. Now, whenever you're ready, lie back."

After the medical exam, Dr. Wei gives me a slip of paper with her signature—a referral to a radiologist and, if necessary, a breast oncologist—and I slip it into that special little high-up pocket of my tote bag, but I don't do anything about it for a while.

If I don't go to the doctor, then we can't know for sure if something is wrong. The not knowing I can deal with. Being in the dark is, apparently, a state I'm used to. Before I go to the specialists, it can be both biting and banal. Schrödinger's Tumor.

The referral goes into the top drawer of my desk, where I know no one will look.

*

After my mother died, I went to the same bar every night. It was the step-down kind, where you feel like you're in a little cave. There was a red neon sign in the window with the bar's name, and a chalkboard sign out front announcing its generous happy hour. A real draw. And it was sort of on my way home from my work at the time.

Also, it was a bar that my mom and I had accidentally stumbled into one evening, when we were holiday shopping in the neighborhood and I really had to pee—something she mocked me for. "You have a weak bladder," she observed, as we stepped down into the dark. "You're sure you want to go *here?*"

But the bar had pizza, which we split. My mom had a weakness for melted cheese. "It's your fault, you know," she chided. "When I was pregnant with you"—she poked at me here—"all I wanted was pizza. Extra. Cheese. Pizza. For *days.*"

The day after I lost my mom, I found myself back at this bar. It had been years since we were there, but the bar was, miraculously, exactly as it had been. In a comforting way—not in the sad way that her house was, as I returned to clear it weekend after weekend. The bar was kind of like a secret routine because it wasn't a place she would normally be, so nothing reminded me too much of her. I could just have this one contained memory without the weight of a bunch of other ones. It could be this one simple thing.

On the first night, I went alone. On the second night, Darlene offered to come with me but I vehemently refused. Both nights, I ordered a margherita pizza—same as my mom and I had—and ate my half and took her half to go. I picked at it over lunch the next day. It was like meal prep. I thought: if I just did this every day, for a while—maybe even forever—that would be okay.

And on the third night, I met Sam. Sam, who was charismatic and kind, who made me feel at ease, somehow, for the first time in days. Sam, who made me feel like my loss wasn't the most interesting thing about me then. Who felt like he could be the right person at the right time. Who laughed when I made fun of him (for the way he only got down half a shot at a time) and who could dish it right back. Like maybe the universe was sending me family when I needed it most.

*

My son is at the age when he takes his obsession with one small thing and makes it big. He has learned to generalize.

When his obsession was dinosaurs two years ago, we took him to visit the natural history museum. It was a big day. Father and son, palms leaving prints against the train window as we crossed over the bridge. My husband believed you could tell how good a day it was going to be based on how sparkly the water was. There was a definite shine then. My daughter was asleep on my lap, a weighted blanket.

At the museum, my son read every sign. He was six then, so we were there awhile. He insisted on taking photos in front of every dinosaur. My husband had him pose like he was readying himself for a battle. We got him a plush brontosaurus from the gift shop. (I can only think of how I later learned that the brontosaurus was fake; they decided the bones belonged to a different type of dinosaur altogether and stripped the beloved long-neck of its existence. I knew how it felt. But *then* they realized they had been mistaken and restored its title. I wish science would make up its mind.)

All the way home, my son was a fountain of facts. The comparisons were the thing that blew his mind: a *T. rex* is as heavy as this many school buses, consumes the weight of this many kids.

After his museum high ended, lulled by the sway of the train car, Noah fell fast asleep. He had been in the middle of a sentence when he just drifted off, and stayed in that serene state until we arrived at our stop. Sam lifted his boy from the subway and carried him up the stairs. Though Noah was getting a little big for that, Sam made it look so effortless. Being with my husband was like that. Like being a kid, being able to fall asleep on the ride home.

Now, Noah wants to know everything about the trees. I show him the Ents from *Lord of the Rings*, and he is disappointed that they're just make-believe. "Only the real thing," he tells me. He wants to know about places he can put his boots on someday.

*

My daughter is at an age where she always wants to know why: Why are we doing this? Why are we going here? Why does Daddy have to go to work? Why can't he stay? (This one guts me.)

And then, like a four-year-old philosopher scientist: Why is the sky blue? Why can't we see the stars during the day? I marvel at this splendid creature; where did she come from? She persists: Why is the sun always whole while the moon makes herself into different shapes and shades night after night?

Tonight, when Sam calls from his "business trip" to wish them good night, I insist on being the one and only bedtime story. "Give me that, at least," I say to my husband, who promises. Like my daughter, I've been reaching for whys. I've been trying to pick answers from the worn fabric of our lives like lint. So I attempt to answer her last question, the one about the moon, the best way I can.

Tonight, I make a show of pulling back the window curtains, so we can peer out and up at the setting where this story takes place. My daughter slumps into her pillow mound, ready to be entertained. As I take my place at the foot of her bed, I marvel at how much she's grown, how little space there is for me now. My son sits at the edge of his own bed, listening but distinctly separate from us. There's a thin smear of cinnamon toothpaste in the left corner of his mouth, and I resist the urge to wipe it off.

Tonight, the moon is mostly full, which is perfect for our purposes. The best possible visual aid. It's round and plump, bright except in some patches, where it glows more dimly, like it's covered in a thin layer of soot.

I point this out, and my daughter reiterates her question: "Why?"

I ask them for their theories first.

"The moon is cheese and cows ate some of it."

"The moon is cheese that has gone bad."

"The moon is a man's face with moon chicken pox."

"Maybe," I tell them.

"Well, what do you think, Mom?" my daughter asks.

It's a story my own mother told me, when I was probably Noah's age and obsessed with the night sky and its secrets. She would always try to map her stories onto what I was learning in school. I went on about the sun and the planets, each with its distinct moons. And my mom—always a bit of a troublemaker, always a touch mischievous in small ways—told me that I should ask my teacher about the tree on the moon . . .

I'm surprised by how quickly it returns. Like a song you didn't know you still knew all the words to, the way you always instinctively remember your childhood address, your first phone number. Almost like muscle memory, pulling your credit card from your wallet without having to rifle through the slots, or your maiden name always at the tip of your tongue. Ingrained. The things cut into you at an early age, the ones closest to the core of who you are.

"On the moon, there's a tree," I tell them. I watch for my son's reaction, see that he's leaned slightly forward. "A really big, beautiful tree. The most beautiful tree you've ever seen. Sturdy. Tall. And the dappled shade that dances across the surface is actually its shadow. And on the moon, there's also a man."

"Is he the most beautiful man?" my daughter guesses, and I laugh.

"No, he's actually pretty average. But he was sent there as a punishment by the gods. Banished from our planet. And the gods tell him that he has to cut down the tree. That's part of his punishment.

So the pretty average man spends all night cutting down this tree. And in the morning, he thinks he's done. He thinks it was easy. That maybe he can come home now. But by the next night, much to his surprise, the tree has grown itself back again. It's a magic tree. And so he starts over. He spends all night cutting down this tree again. And the next night, there it stands. And the cycle never stops. He's stuck there for all of eternity."

"What kind of tree can grow back that quickly? And how did it grow on the moon?" my son demands.

"What did he do?"

"Stories for another day," I tell them.

I tuck them both in, shut the lights, and close the door quietly behind me.

On work nights, my husband has a tendency to go to bed at an ungodly hour. The early bird gets the worm, but I've always been more of a night owl. In this way, for a while now, it has felt like we don't sleep in the same bed.

Our kids' room is right by the stairs, so I take a seat at the top. After our first child was born, we decided to carpet the staircase, despite sort of hating carpet. We chose a very neutral beige, hoping it would blend in with the light wood of the banister. We got the thickest, fluffiest carpet we could. We were so afraid of edges then.

Still, the carpet feels nice on my bare feet. I scrunch my toes up. It's a comfortable spot. I can hear the exasperated whine of the twin frames as my kids burrow into their beds. I think of the old baby monitors, the way we had to listen carefully to catch every sound, every hiccup or possible missed breath. Now, here they are: enough weight in the world to make furniture creak under their turning bodies.

On my phone, I google the myth my mother told me, mindful

of the gaps in my memory. What kind of tree was it, anyway? And what did the pretty average man do to piss off the gods so much that they'd exile him?

Of course, there are several versions of the story.

In the simplest one, dating back to the ninth century, there isn't a lot of context: just the image of this one man cutting down this one tree for all of eternity.

In another version, there is (what do you know?) an affair. The man's name is Wu Gang, and one day, he comes home to find his wife carrying on an affair with the Fire Emperor's grandson. In a fit of rage, Wu Gang murders his wife's lover, which the emperor isn't too thrilled about for obvious reasons.

Or, Wu Gang wishes to ascend to Taoist immortality, but he's also sort of lazy and gives up. (I find this version most relatable.) For his disrespect, the Jade Emperor punishes him with this impossible and unending task.

In yet another variation, Wu Gang is a woodcutter, working with a teacher in the mountains to reach a level of immortality. He gives up easily in this version, too, and so his teacher sends him to the moon as a lesson in patience and discipline. Devotion.

Of course the demeanor of the moon (a feminine entity) is determined by the cuts a man makes. The wield of the ax. Cherry trees and lying.

*

The first time I heard that story was at the Chinese beauty salon. Well, one of them. There were many in the neighborhood where I grew up: at times, two or three to a single city block. They competed for talent constantly, boasting when they had poached a stylist by taping a neon oaktag sign to the window, with the words: _____ IS HERE.

My mom followed Sindy, her favorite stylist, from salon to salon. She followed her the way some people follow rock bands, or religion. In a sense, all the salons were the same. They used the same bright red hair-cutting capes and dingy purple towels and brands of hair spray. The haircuts were cheap, cash only, and the people there were brusque with their customers. They were blunt and made you wait and sat their friends first and gossiped about the ones they didn't like in dialects they knew the clientele didn't understand. It was one of our favorite places on earth.

When you got there, they handed you a big book of washed-out photographs with outdated hairstyles to flip through, the pages brittle and bleached by the sun. This was especially useful in the case of a language barrier: we watched so many white women breeze in for a quick blowout. All they had to do was point and become, like magic.

Of course, there were other times, when they got exasperated with their hairstylists; when they spoke curtly and slowly like they were speaking to a child; when they got loud, as though increasing the sheer volume of their voice would fill in the gaps of communication between them. At times like these, my mother would turn my attention to this other book they kept in the waiting area: the book of hair. It was full of colorful, tactile samples, little loops of real hair that were organized by gradation: blonds and brunettes and reds and grays all tucked in their place. You could hold a curl of your new color in your hand, hold it up to your face, see how it changed in the light. As a child, the book of hair grossed me out and fascinated me in equal measure. All these selves you could put on.

Every few months when I was growing up, I would go with my mom and wait while she got her hair dyed—one of the few luxuries she afforded herself. Sindy would pull a little plastic chair up just for me, and I would hold my mom's purse and watch as the paste was worked through. And then Sindy would get pulled into other conversations, start chatting with other clients, and we would wait for the dye to set, for the grays to be gone. We would wait for it to turn back time.

While we waited, my mom would tell me these stories. Fairy tales, myths she remembered her mother telling her a long time ago. When I was little, I used to think it was something in the dye that made her reminisce, like a spell she had fallen under. In hindsight, she was probably just trying to keep me from being bored or complaining about the stench of the chemicals. But I hung on every word.

It became a kind of sacred ritual for us. For me, it was a rare window of time alone with my mother—a window that let me peer into her otherwise private past a little more. This treasured time, when it was me and my mom and her stories. And there was the way my mom looked when her hair was just done. When Sindy stepped back from her work and waited for us at the register, there was the way my mom smiled quietly to herself, shook her curls from side to side to see how they moved. She looked younger, maybe. More vibrant. For just an instant, she looked like she recognized herself. Even now, I cannot untangle the passing down of these stories and the ability to recognize yourself somewhere in the retelling. It's like I have wed the two in my mind, convinced myself that the act of sharing these stories might salvage something of your truest self.

*

Lily has a favorite joke that no one else is allowed to tell. She heard it once at school, and now she repeats it nearly every morning: There were two muffins sitting in the oven. One pops up and says, "Oh boy—it's hot in here!" and the other pops up and says, "Oh boy—a talking muffin!"

She laughs and laughs at the absurdity, at breaking the rules you didn't know were there.

*

In my early twenties, when a group of us would gather at a bar after work on a casual Thursday, fueled by happy-hour-priced spicy margaritas, I found that the conversation would eventually wind itself down one of two paths: (1) the bottom of the ocean (particularly popular if the *Washington Post* had recently published something about the emergence of a big, ugly fish we hadn't seen in a while) or (2) the possibility of motherhood.

"Do you want kids?" a friend would ask, and I would think, sure, I've held a baby once before—and successfully! So I'd say, "Yeah, maybe, someday," while nodding and looking wistfully into the middle distance for a short period of time before someone's favorite song playing in the background would inevitably reach its chorus and we'd all be singing along, and that would be that.

But the older you get, the more you realize that that question houses so many other questions. Questions about the state of the world and where you can truthfully see yourself in it. After the vague notion of being okay with kids on a philosophical level— the acknowledgment that you are not, say, repulsed or morally opposed on the grounds of the environment, overpopulation, or on behalf of orphans—there is the reckoning with your lot in life. Your financial reality. Your body's limitations.

If you have a uterus, you might consider the daily toll on it. There is the prospect of eating lots of food and getting fat with abandon (a plus). There is also the fact that you can't have alcohol or sushi for many, many months (a big minus).

Also, the pain. The pain was something I was morbidly curious about. The first to have a baby in a friend group is bombarded with questions. We want to know exactly how much it hurts, on a scale of one to ten. We want her to compare the pain to something we all know—cramps, rib tattoos, appendicitis, broken bones—and then we find we have startlingly little in common in the ways things hurt.

For me, there was the question of whether I could bring a baby into the world who looked like me; who I could not protect from casual racism; who I was certain would one day step into a classroom with a kid who would mockingly tug at the corners of their own eyes; who I knew would have people guessing what country they were *really* from all their life; who would, more likely than not, hurt in the same small ways I had hurt. To this, my white friends would *mmm* thoughtfully and say, "Fair," though it was anything but.

I remember the first time the kids question bubbled up between my husband and me. We were dating somewhat seriously then. It was a weekend. We were milling around the farmers' market. There was a redheaded child in front of us, and he was touching all the plums. *Squeezing* all the plums. He was clutching two mangled plum carcasses in his palms, and there was plum juice running down the sides of his forearms. Honestly, he just looked generally sticky, the way that most small children do. I remember his mother turning around and noting with a mixture of horror and exhaustion what her progeny had been up to in the millisecond that her back had been turned. We watched as she took the plums, gently, from his palms, held them gingerly between her thumbs and pointer fingers, and marched up to the register, apologizing profusely.

Something I've heard a few people say after having a baby: "My heart now lives permanently outside of my body." The heart being the child. The idea being that your heart is no longer yours; it has agency and is out of your control. But that day at the farmers' market, I remember thinking that having a kid would also be a lot like having your embarrassment live outside of your body. And I, personally, do enough to embarrass myself on a daily basis. I could not imagine letting an entity capable of embarrassing me just walk around like that.

But then the kid was so sorry, he kept saying it—to the farmer manning the register, to his mom as they strolled away. And he was just so genuine in his emotion in a way that made it kind of okay. Or at least in a way that fascinated me.

So when my not-yet-husband, who was also witnessing this theater of remorse, had asked me, cautiously, "Would you want kids someday?" despite all of the above, I said, "Yeah, maybe, someday," and meant it.

And when that someday came around—after I had answered yes to all the big ones, like "Will you marry me?" and "Do you take this man?" and "Do you think it's time to start trying?"—I found there are more questions still. There are the obvious ones, the ones that people hurl at you. Everyone asking urgently, "Is it a boy or a girl?" and "What are you going to name him?"

And still, settled there like sediment beneath a boulder, there are questions that aren't so much about the child as they are about ourselves. There are a lot of stupid online quizzes you can take about what type of parent you'll be.

For instance, will you be the type of parent who tells the truth about Santa Claus? The tooth fairy? The birds and the bees and death? Have you thought about it? Which lies you're willing to tell?

*

Santa Claus existed for my husband longer than he did for most other kids. Whereas most children start to see the sheen of make-believe tarnish around the age of, let's say, eight, Sam went on believing for many years after that—till nearly puberty. Honestly, there is a small part of me that suspects he harbors that belief still. It fuels his boyish charm. This, I think, is emblematic of Sam's crystalline childhood. His whole youth was spent in a splendid puppet theater that existed solely for his entertainment. He was its lone audience member, and his mother was the one pulling the strings.

This past year was probably the last one in which Santa (and his friends the tooth fairy and the Easter Bunny) could waltz freely through our home. Because Noah, my smart boy, is starting to ask questions. He came home from school that first day back from winter recess, and he looked at me like never before: with suspicion. Kids talk. He waited until his little sister had left the room for a second (a small kindness) and asked me if Santa had really given him his new bike *for real.* Sam and I hadn't ever really discussed what to do in situations like these; we had never decided on the appropriate age for disbelief. We stood there in silence for a minute, till Lily came whooshing back into the room, new Christmas dolls in tow.

Shortly after that, Sam's parents—the Moores—came for a visit. They were on their way to Key West, where they were going to wait out the rest of the winter. Sam's mother was asking Noah how he was liking his gifts from Santa, and he must have given her a somewhat snarky (or, at the very least, skeptical) response because the very next day, my phone rang and it was Mrs. Moore. She views Noah's disbelief in Santa as a personal failing of mine. She views me as a woman who can't keep magic alive in her own home.

Sam's mother likes to stick to a script. She doesn't appreciate plot twists. (This is why she reads and rereads and rereads the Holy Bible: she already knows how everything is going to turn out.) When she has you over for dinner, everything feels a little rehearsed.

She loves packaging words up into people's mouths. Telling them when to let the sentences out, like a marionette operator or a symphony conductor. Actually, this is how Noah got his favorite joke. It was stored in him for safekeeping by his grandmother. He only pulls it out at parties, when prompted by her: How do you make holy water? You boil the hell out of it.

*

When Sam returned from Oyster Bay, I was prepared to tell him about the possibility of the cancer. Telling him would make it real, but he would make it okay. In hindsight, I think that's why I waited to do anything about it.

Sam had a way of making life easy. Yes, the family money also did that. It obliterated big obstacles, and it gave him the confidence and peace of mind that allowed him to take care of little things like *that*. While someone like me would spiral endlessly about the greater implications of bad news, to the point of being unable to make the first phone call—Sam could just pick up the phone.

I would tell him later, after the kids were asleep. He would hold my hand as we called the radiologist. He would write down the date and time and address. He would take the day off for once and accompany me to my mammogram appointment. He would take care of everything. He would take notes and know the next steps. He would schedule a biopsy, a surgery, if necessary. He would get the name of the best doctors; he would pay for the best care team. All I would have to do was be shepherded through doorways.

The kids were ecstatic about his homecoming. He'd only been gone for a week, but they were *so* happy to see him that it was hard not to take it a little personally. I listened to them snort and chortle from my perch in the hallway when he gave an encore storytelling session that involved Strega Nona lost in the world of *Cloudy with a Chance of Meatballs*. I waited downstairs with a cannonball in my stomach, knowing that what I was about to tell him could take all that laughter away. I had never felt farther away from the three of them.

When Sam came downstairs, we sat in the kitchen. He poured us some wine, and when he handed me my glass, that's when I realized he wasn't wearing his wedding ring.

"I've been doing some thinking, and I think I'm going to try to find a new place. I think that'll be best. I'll be here, for a bit, while I'm looking, but I'll stay out of your way," he said, like someone who had caused me a minor inconvenience and not someone who cracked our lives wide open.

When I looked at him, I could tell that he genuinely thought he was doing the right thing. Sam was always someone who was good at fully living inside his body, inside his emotions, inside the moment he found himself in. You could tell that he was raised on "following your heart" and "being true to yourself." It was something I used to love about him, the way that he so freely inhabited the present. Now, of course, this earnest search for bliss and self seemed flighty in a way I had never considered before.

But I suppose I did know, even from that first conversation at the restaurant, that "I'm having an affair" had already hardened into "I'm leaving you." Because he was *sorry* but did not ask for my forgiveness. That's how you know when someone has more or less made up their mind about what they're going to do without you.

It became clear when my husband came home that there was another timeline that I was a part of but not privy to. His relationship had already calcified.

I felt the lump in my chest, and I thought about the other new timeline that my life might be beholden to.

*

Before I make the first appointment, I have a plan. I make up a lot of excuses in my head, plugs for the holes in my day, stories to explain long stretches of absence in case my husband should care enough to ask. (He doesn't.)

It's a shame, too, because I concocted some pretty magnificent lies about where I had been—and, yes, why. I'd do this clever thing where I'd mention a PTA mom's upcoming birthday very intentionally in passing, right after dinner but before the plates were cleared, because it was when I knew he would be paying the most attention. Before dinner, everyone is so focused on being fed. And once cleanup begins, it's all about the mental maze of the dishwasher and not being the one to absolutely fill the trash can, lest you be tasked with taking it out. It's a delicate dance, and more demanding than you might expect. Anyway, the birthday comment was great because you could squeeze two excuses out of it: one day to purchase the present and another for the brunch. Two for the price of one. I'm a very economical liar.

A few years ago, in the days leading up to Christmas, my husband and I realized our son's main present was going to be delayed. My husband fretted and fretted over this, because the remote-control car had been his idea, and he had special-ordered it. It was going to be the first time our son was disappointed on Christmas morning, and we were so wrapped up in what we could procure in a night that we completely forgot he had also lost a baby tooth, politely biting into his grandmother's fruitcake after dinner. When morning came, and there was no change under his pillow and no bow-wrapped present for him under the tree, I simply told him that there had been a (minor) traffic accident in the sky. In their haste to get to him and all the other children, Santa's sled and the tooth fairy collided. Luckily, they were both fine, and he could expect delivery in the next three to five business days.

See: the threads coming together, like the end of a *Seinfeld* episode.

Despite everything (or, perhaps, precisely because of it), I wanted to put the least possible number of lies into the atmosphere of our home, like they were exhaust fumes that would be bad to breathe in, that could stunt growth.

In the middle of the day when no one is home, I sit on my perch in the stairwell and call the doctor. We set a date for the mammogram.

*

Darlene wants me to write a list of all my least favorite things about Sam. It's something we used to do in college. Whenever either of us would start dating someone, we kept a secret little list of everything we kind of hated about them. That way, when things inevitably did not turn out in our favor, we could point to our list and say we were better off.

Sam and I met after this silly and childish bit had run its course, so there was no list for him. But here it is:

If he's not in his work button-downs, he's always wearing his Ivy League college sweatshirt.

He's always misplacing his keys. (Admittedly, I used to think it was cute that I could always find them, but maybe, psychologically, this flaw revealed his reluctance to come home.)

He does that rich people thing in restaurants where he folds the receipt in half, so you can't see how much he tipped.

He is so generous in volunteering to run to the store, but he seldom comes back with what you asked for. (Flowers instead of flour.)

He doesn't so much walk as he glides. He moves through the world with an obliviousness that I mistook for optimism.

In the waiting room, Darlene and I pass the time by adding to the list, making it grow.

On my turn: "He leaves empty wrappers everywhere."

On hers: "He actively *chooses* to get his coffee at Starbucks over all the actually good coffee shops in the city."

Darlene is a really good friend because she is soft-launching her disdain. I know that if she had it her way, we'd be calling him and cursing him out; prank calling the other woman. We'd be slashing his tires and egging his car. Trying to put a hex on him under the light of the full moon—that kind of thing. Instead, Darlene lets her hatred come out in these small, safe ways.

While less close acquaintances might be quick to say, "Fuck him!" and launch into a monologue about how they never really liked him in the first place, Darlene understands that it's more complicated than that. Because she knows there was good, too. Because of Noah and Lily—all the manifestation of that good. She can still see some version of love buried just there, so she knows we can't write him off or write him out completely. We just have to find new ways of writing the story.

"He loves movie sequels with an unchecked passion."

"Didn't he not know sloths were real animals until, like, a year ago?"

This one makes me laugh. It's true: Sam thought sloths were made-up creatures like unicorns—in fact, he *insisted*—until Noah showed him a *National Geographic* issue that proved otherwise. It makes me feel better, playing this game with Darlene in the worst room in the world. It takes us someplace else, back to our college days and away from the absurdity of this very adult situation. In a sick way, it is a good distraction. Our game shrinks Sam down to these very bite-size tidbits: the kind of thing you'd find on the back of a kid's cereal box or on the intro index card taped to a dog's cage at the shelter. *This is SAM. SAM is mostly affectionate and bad at fetch; he always brings back the wrong things.*

*

"It's an osmanthus tree, by the way," I tell my son. "On the moon, in that myth. I looked it up for you. They don't heal themselves quite like in the story, but people use them in Chinese medicine all the time. They're supposed to be cleansing."

"Cool," he says, barely looking up from his bowl of breakfast cereal.

Sometimes being a mother feels like a punishment out of myth. The tree that won't accept its severance from the ground. The stone being rolled up the hill. (The stone stuck in my chest.)

*

Waiting for your name to be called in doctors' offices is such a strange thing. You both want and do not want to hear it. On the one hand, you'd love to get this over with as quickly as possible so you can go home and eat the leftover takeout Massaman curry in the fridge. On the other hand, you want to put it off as long as humanly possible.

When they call my name, I stand up because I recognize the sound of it, but it has never sounded so foreign to me, so far away or so little like something I want to claim.

They let Darlene come with me to the next room, the second waiting room. She's insistent on going as far as she can. She doesn't even ask permission. "They'll stop me if I'm somewhere I'm really not supposed to be," she reasons. Every time, she just jumps right up when they say my name, like it's her own.

It reminds me of attending these appointments with my own mother; they let me in every room because I was both her translator and her daughter. When Darlene was asked what our relationship was, she said, "I'm her sister," without skipping a beat, for fear that they would kick her out if she wasn't a blood relative.

In the second space, I'm asked to change. The thing I remember most about all these appointments is the paper robe. The paper robe is thin and drafty and crinkles every time you shift your weight. The paper robe is terribly unflattering. It lies flat across you, washes you in an awful sickly white. It makes a blank box of you.

The nurse offers me the key to a small locker for my things, but I decline because Darlene is there to guard my valuables. I don't remember folding my clothes, but that's the way I hand them to my friend. We go into the next waiting room and sit with its soft, smooth jazz for a little while. There are three other women sitting here, each alone. All older. They look at us with a tight-smile pity that surely has to do with age. I know what they're thinking: *What are they doing here?* For a moment, under their gaze, I feel impossibly young.

One by one, we go off into the exam room as summoned. With different music, it would be a horror movie. When it's my turn, the nurse reminds me that I should take off all my jewelry, just in case. I mentally scan my body, in the tune of that one children's song that Lily's been singing lately: head, shoulders, knees, etc. I press each piece into Darlene's waiting palms: small gold studs, a necklace with a citrine crystal that the "kids" got me for my birthday last year, and—my wedding ring. As good a time as any to take it off. As it leaves my finger, I notice there is an impression there, as though it's been a little tight. Darlene sees it, too. She closes her palm around the gold band, and we don't say anything about it. After all, there is no time for sentiment; the nurse is waiting at the doorway.

"Good luck!" Darlene calls after us. Her voice sounds limp in the corridor. The rest, I must do alone. Luckily, I'm not in the room for a terribly long time before the radiologist pops in.

"My hands are going to be a little cold," she apologizes, and then she squeezes and pokes and prods at my chest. I focus on keeping myself as still as possible. I try to keep myself out of my body. Truthfully, I'm a terribly ticklish person, and when she feels at the sides close to my armpits, I'm afraid I'm going to burst out laughing. "I'm ticklish," I warn her. "Most people are," she says reassuringly.

Once she has identified the lump in question, she begins the ultrasound. The gel is cool on my skin. The goose bumps ripple up. She moves her wand around. She takes screenshots, makes notes in her chart, but shares nothing. It is the opposite of my first sonogram, my husband at my side, something good growing. I'm host to something terrible now. My body turned.

"We're going to do the needle biopsy now," she says. "Please hold as still as you can. You're doing great." I do as she says. I want to be the stillest a patient has ever been. I don't watch; I keep my eyes trained on the ceiling, but I can feel the pressure—the jolt of something being taken away from me.

She says they'll call with the results in the next week or so. I find Darlene waiting, in the designated room. And I have never been more relieved to see her. This is the first time I look at my best friend and see her as someone who could really raise my kids if it came to that. A very good substitute. Better than me, even. They would run around with her dog, who would learn to love them! Darlene would show them how to make ceramics! She would let them paint their rooms whatever color they wanted! It could be a nice life.

She hands me back my clothes and my treasures. I take everything but the ring back. "Would you hang on to this for me, for a little while?"

"Of course," Darlene says, and she slips it back into her purse without another word.

It is a painfully beautiful day: one of, like, five perfect days we'll get all season. Or maybe the world just feels more colorful by comparison, outside those sterile rooms. My ring finger feels so naked; I can't help but run my thumb over the spot where my ring used to be, over and over.

We go to a nearby burrito place and get frozen margaritas. They told me not to drink for twenty-four hours, so I just take little sips from Darlene's cup. At one point, I cut my tongue on the salt along the rim, and blood fills my mouth. For once, we have very little to say to one another. I have an overwhelming urge to cry, and I can't pinpoint where it's coming from. I look at Darlene through my own misty eyes, and her eyes are a little watery, too. We blame our allergies. It is, after all, the end of April, and the tulips and the hyacinths are in fine form. I've always liked that the flowers bloom in waves; they wait their turn.

Eventually, I ask, "Would you teach my kids how to throw clay?" as though we were picking up in the middle of a conversation. Darlene, who knows me, does not need context. She knows what I mean. "Absolutely," she says with a finality that soothes me. Every room becomes a waiting room.

*

One morning, sometime after the secret biopsy, I'm awoken by the specific *shhh* of kids trying to keep each other quiet. They're in the hallway, outside my bedroom door. Sam isn't next to me; I'm alone. Right.

It's genuinely quiet for maybe one second, and then I hear them go, "One, two, three!" The door pushes open, and there they are in the room with me, screaming, "Happy Mother's Day!!" No matter what happens, this will always be my day. There is relief and sorrow there. Even if my husband remarries, this will *still* be my day primarily, and no one can rob me of it. If I die, it will be a void on the calendar for my kids for all their years to come.

But today, they bound into the bed full of life, with construction-paper cards and these dinky little fragile flowers in disposable grow pots that they bought at the PTA sale at school yesterday. (I can say that—I helped organize it.)

Sam trails behind with orange juice and McDonald's hotcakes and hash browns on a tray. "Happy Mother's Day," he says, and it's so weird how it sounds the same as it does every year.

Noah and Lily fight over whose card I'm going to read first. They're telling me that they love me—that I'm the best mom ever, the best mom in the entire world, the whole universe!!—and even though I know this is a completely unfounded statement, it sounds so true coming out of their perfect little mouths. I want so badly to morph into this fabulous mother for them.

They're clutching these delicate little flowers and handing them to me like it's the entirety of their love. "Do you like it, Mom? Mom?" They want to know. They keep asking. Noah's got this very sweet bunch of pink petunias with the petals mostly still intact. Lily gives me a celosia, one of those fuzzy little guys that looks like it's been plucked straight out of Dr. Seuss's hands. These flowers are going to die by the end of the season (if not sooner). They're annuals, which means they don't come back.

"Yellow, your favorite," Lily says proudly, and her remembering this tidbit about me means more than I can say.

*

The body positions my children take to naturally in slumber really pull back the curtain. Not an accidental dropping of limbs but a careful arrangement that says an awful lot about them. Personally, I'm a side sleeper: one arm crooked under the pillow and my knees bent up toward my chest. My husband used to make fun of me for this. A little armadillo, he'd call me. All balled up for battle. I don't think he liked that I slept turned away from him most nights. My body, a concave. Like I was trying to take up as little space as possible.

Standing in their room, checking on them before I turn in for the night, and I am surprised to find that my daughter sleeps like me. I try not to read too much into this.

My husband sleeps flat on his back, a deceptive openness.

My son is a stomach sleeper, starfished out over everything. His limbs hang off the bed like aerial roots trying to touch the soil once more. For a while, when he was a few years younger, he had a problem with rolling out of the bed in the dead of night. We'd taken him to a sleep specialist, who could find nothing wrong with him. "A bigger bed?" she'd suggested. "Make sure he always has the bottom bunk if he goes to camp." Eventually, he grew out of the habit. Subconsciously, he learned to find the edges, to know his own tipping point. Still, with his arms dangling over like that, it looked like his body would always be attempting to find ground.

*

Sometimes I wonder how Maggie sleeps. Not in a holier-than-thou *how does she sleep at night* kind of way, but genuinely: What does it feel like to be her, to sleep in a bed with Sam when you are not his wife?

To be in the swaddle of new love—does it turn you into a different sleeper, or are you the most yourself when you are sleeping?

Does Sam curl in toward you? (In love like parentheses.) I try so hard to conjure this feeling. But I'm on the outside of it now.

*

"I want to know everything about Maggie," I declare one morning. "Are you sure?" Darlene cautions, pouring syrup over her French toast. We're at a new restaurant on my corner, eating breakfast.

"The not-knowing is worse," I say. That's what I've decided. The powers of my imagination know no bounds. The realities are probably (fingers crossed!) far more pedestrian than anything I could torture myself with. Plus, it will be a pretty good distraction from the fact that I haven't heard back from the doctor.

So we dive into Maggie, scroll through her public past. Maybe if I know that her favorite movie is *Breakfast at Tiffany's*; that her favorite band is the Killers and that she has seen them twice in concert; that she bakes for birthdays; that she captions her photos with quotes from books she probably hasn't read; that her parents have retired to Virginia with a little white dog named Marshmallow; that her younger brother is on the spectrum and that they are very close; that she volunteers at a food kitchen, but maybe only around the holidays; that she has once run the New York City Marathon;

that she studied abroad in Argentina; that she went to one pasta-making class; that she sometimes does yoga on the weekends; that she loves Lambrusco and fresh daisies and ordering pizza on Fridays from the same place I order my pizza from—maybe, if I know all these things about her, it feels somehow less special that Sam knows these things, too.

I have in my mind that finding these things out might rob them of their intimacy in some small way. I want to know everything about her, so she feels less like a secret and more like something I am let in on. Less like another door that has been closed to me.

*

I've been thinking about the stories I have and have not passed down to my kids. Up until recently, I've been content to read someone else's printed words, but these days, I'm wanting to give them more of myself for safekeeping. I decide to tell my children a different race story, one that has a hare but no tortoise. This is the story of the animals on the Chinese zodiac, and the competition that decided their order. Before we begin, I remind my children of their place in this world, because I want them to find themselves in the story: my son, the energetic and fun-loving monkey. My daughter, the clever rat. This upsets her. "I don't want to be a rat!" she chants, close to tears. She's likely picturing the things that run wild and wet in the subway tunnels, the things people recoil from in the street late at night. "What if we called it a mouse?" Her brother tries to soothe her. "You could be Minnie, with the pink bow." She shakes her head furiously. Of course I'm ruining story time already. "You know, your father was born in the year of the rat, too," I tell her, and this quiets her.

They let me begin: To determine the order of the zodiac signs, a race was designed. All the animals on the earth were invited, but only twelve animals arrived at the starting line. The Jade Emperor promised them each a place, and the competition would decide their rightful order.

Part of the course involved a river, which every creature had to cross. "Can rats swim?" my youngest wants to know. "I can't swim yet," she says, wide-eyed with concern. I ruffle her bangs. I tell her, "Oh, don't worry. The clever rat jumps on the back of the strong ox, and the ox carries him across to safety. The rat jumps off at the last second and wins the race." My daughter cheers, "I win! I win!" She raises her arms above her head.

"Is that allowed?" my son wants to know.

"It's not *not* allowed," I say. "All's fair."

I tell the rest of the story, the roll call of the animals. As I'm leaving, my daughter asks, "Which one are you?"

I whisper, so quietly I'm not sure she even hears me, "The ox." Second place.

*

They just have so much in *common*—that's what Sam tells me, when prodded. That's the reason he fell. Like looking into a mirror, like staring at a reflection, like Narcissus all over again.

(They had even, they discovered, summered in neighboring houses on the Cape during the same month during the same year when they were children. It would be one of those cute stories you read about on the internet. There might even be a photo in some attic taken of Sam with her lurking prophetically in the background.)

It was like she was some missing piece in his life. Like I was a door to some wider world, and she was the door back into his own house. Someone his mother would love.

Sam and I often talked about our different upbringings. Race, class—these have always been out-loud parts of our relationship. It's something I liked about us. It's something I would point to and say, *"This."* We could talk about anything in this skewed world we had been handed. We could talk and talk and get under each other's skin in the ways that only a lover can.

But none of that would be necessary with Maggie. No explanations required. Maggie comes from his world. The world of rules that you just have to *know* and abide by. The rules about the right opinions and how to say them, the right clothes, the right fork choice. The fork in the road, and so he chose.

*

I'm lying across Darlene's couch with my head on the cushion and my legs dangling from the armrest. Lily loves sitting like this, and honestly, I can see why. Roberta is sitting between us, with one paw on her owner at all times. Darlene's dog has terrible separation anxiety. The dog trainer says she needs to make hellos and goodbyes less of a big deal. It should be expected that people come and go like that. Darlene is fixated on her laptop.

"What do you think she's like in bed?" I ask.

"Terrible!" she says, not looking up from the screen.

"Terrible how?" I ask.

She gives me an exasperated sigh. "She looks like a real pillow princess," Darlene says eventually. "She lies there like a dead fish! Doesn't move her hips. She fakes orgasms, but in that way that guys like?" she ventures, laughing and mimicking the exaggerated sound. Then, softer, "Can we focus, please?"

Darlene has actually called me here so she can read to me from the pages of notes she's been taking on breast cancer. My best friend is better at having a body. She knows what to feed it, and how much sleep it requires. She exercises it religiously. She goes to the doctor for well visits, likes the reassurance of people—experts—telling her that she's going to be okay. She doesn't like men, doesn't let them near her, doesn't let them in—we joke that this improves her health overall.

Darlene has been up late reading horror stories, worst-case scenarios, but she spares me the details. She asks intimate, attentive questions about the tumor's size and willingness to be moved. It weighs like a small skipping stone in my right breast. It can be coaxed a centimeter to either side. (Darlene says this is good. It's the fixed ones, the stubborn ones, we need to fret over.)

Then she asks something new. She asks if she can touch it. To see if it feels like a grape, the way they say it will. (It doesn't. It feels like a lump. The thing that gets caught in your throat when someone you love says something terrible.) I pin down the spot for her, the way I will for all our friends who will ask, who spin my life into their own cautionary tale. Feel it here. Here is the hard part.

*

The language of these big life moments isn't quite right: the way we talk about people who have "lost" their lives. The battle against a cruel disease: a war in which there are no real winners. If you die of cancer, does it make you a loser? It implies a lack of strength, or otherwise a kind of carelessness I cannot reckon with. It robs you of your agency in a way that reminds me of "losing" your virginity.

(My college put on its own version of *The Vagina Monologues*, and my submission went something like: "I didn't lose my virginity; I know exactly where I put it.")

*

There are so many people that come with sickness. So many doctors and nurses and specialists and second opinions, pharmacists and insurance representatives, waiting room acquaintances and support groups and friends who want you to call their friends who've been through the same thing. I barely like meeting new people under normal circumstances, so one can imagine the social anxiety that comes with this, too.

But the person I find I most want to speak to—but can't—is my mother, who lost her life to the same greedy disease years ago. Even if she were alive, I'm not sure what she'd say. When she was still with us, we didn't talk a lot about our emotions, not able to find the shared words for them. It was like having a mountain range inside you, with no way of getting it out: not that you didn't have the artistic ability, but that you were working the details in with invisible ink. It was being able to describe some things: the bigness of the mountains, the fact that there existed birds and trees somewhere. But there was no way to describe all the nooks and crannies, the valleys, the specific shadows and ridges and weird flowers growing up out of nowhere, and footholds. We had no footholds between us.

With her own diagnosis, she kept it a secret for as long as she could. When we spoke about it, when we had to, we spoke about it only in to-do lists, in doctors' appointments and schedules, in medical plans and wills. The facts masked our fear. If we had day-to-day things to discuss—recommended doctors and finalized treatment plans, insurance claims to file and results to fax to other doctors—there would be no room for the less practical things in life. Languishing in one's feelings was frivolous—an activity we could not afford. At least that was how it felt at the time. In this way, we learned to pack our love into the logistics.

I think this is my default setting, too. The love language that is my native tongue. My husband pointed this out to me once, before we were married. "You never say 'I love you' first," he observed, one night, after just having told me he loved me. "But I always say it back!" I protested, always his echo. This is a thing our fights circled around, as if every fight had a mother fight hiding at its core. "Sometimes I really can't tell how you feel." Sam said this a lot in our early months of dating. This puzzled me. I guess Sam was used to women throwing themselves at him, telling him very openly how obsessed they were with him, maybe even writing poetry about it. But hadn't I just spent the past twenty minutes thoroughly cleaning his Brita pitcher with Q-tips? To me, that was an act of love, something that not only said how deeply I cared for his health and time but also implied that I would be back soon to enjoy a nice tall glass of cold, filtered water.

With Noah and Lily, I tried to course-correct. Even before they were born, when they were the size of various fruits in my stomach, I would tell them how much I loved them. Once they were sentient, I said it even more. I wrote it on little notes tucked into their lunch boxes in case they forgot halfway through the day. I said it when they left for school and when they went to sleep, and in this way, "I love you" mostly became a sign-off, a shorthand for *goodbye*.

*

There is another famous race myth: the story of Atalanta, who adamantly opposed the idea of marriage but agreed to wed the suitor who could best her in a footrace. Enter Hippomenes, a man very much in love, who prayed to Aphrodite for help. She gifted him three golden apples, which he was to drop along the way to distract his swift love. In the end, he won the race—and the hand of Atalanta.

It's incredible to me that in all these legends, it's the cunning and the witty that win every single time. Brain over brawn. I find deep comfort in this. Sometimes I feel like I live more in my mind than in my body. Sometimes I worry that this makes me a less available parent.

Kids live so fully in their bodies. They chase their senses with a gusto I no longer have access to. My kids love the way the floor glides beneath their knees as they slide across it. They love the dry crunch of browning leaves and the smoothness of my beaded bracelets. They love the sweet rush of Jell-O, the way it coats their tongues an unnatural color at the end.

I have this photo from the first time they ever tried Berry Blue Jell-O: Noah and Lily and Sam between them, all sticking out their tongues to reveal the blue surprise. It's become a pantry staple in our house. It's Sam's favorite, too. On Jell-O nights, they can often be found on their little bathroom stools, standing on tiptoe and leaning over the sink with their tongues out, absolutely transfixed by the blue on their tongues in the mirror.

Narcissus, Bloody Mary—every fable involving a mirror is really a cautionary tale against vanity. There's this myth my mom used to tell me about mirrors. She said that they were portals to another darker, more chaotic world. She said that our reflections were actually demons—masquerading as mirror images of ourselves while plotting our deaths.

*

Waiting to hear back about the biopsy results feels like the longest week of my life. How did I get back here, to this place where I'm sitting by the phone and waiting for someone to call, for my phone to light up with the glow of possibility? I feel twenty again, thinking every glint of light reflected across its surface is the halo of new information.

I try not to fall down the rabbit hole of WebMD, but sometimes, I have an itch to google something. Instead of obsessing over doctor reviews and rare side effects and survival rates, I stare at the same old photos of Maggie. If it's contained, it can't hurt me. If I go looking for it, surely I must be brave enough to face what I find. But she doesn't update her social media nearly enough for my addictive refreshing these days. When that gets old, I look into the etymology of the word *tumor*. *Tumor* and *tomb*, as it turns out, both hail from the Latin *tumere*, meaning "to swell," and I think it's ironic that these words can convey such fullness and emptiness at once.

*

My husband thinks we should give the kids the best day ever before we tell them about the separation. This he tells me in passing, as he crosses the kitchen into the living room with an armful of blankets. He's been in and out of the Oyster Bay house, but when he's back, he sleeps on the couch. It was a wordless agreement, the kind of thing that was just understood. Later, he will joke that he was voted off the island. On good days, I like this idea of us, as we were. Conjoined, adrift. But that's not really a fair comparison, is it? He chose to kick off. Or maybe it's more like this: I believed it to be an island of us, but how long before he walked the perimeter and realized it was more like a peninsula—with one side attached to some other whole?

After the kids are snuck their second story, he tiptoes downstairs and sets up his makeshift bed. My husband, always the man holding the last secret.

There's a small part of me that wants to fight. Fight for us, I mean. For the kids, for the family. For the picture Noah and Lily had in their heads of us, the crayon renderings of which were hung up all over the house. For the marriage, for the younger version of ourselves who stood in front of a room of people we loved and earnestly made promises we thought we could keep. For the people we were when we met and for the people we thought we could grow into together. For the silly pet names we had for each other. For the shoes we didn't fill. For the doughy, gooey centers of ourselves who melted right into the other person. Weren't we in there somewhere? I have the urge to take Sam by his shoulders and violently shake him till he snaps out of it. I have the urge to knock on his forehead, ask, "Is anybody home?"

But instead, I sit on the ottoman, watch him make parachutes of the sheets. He's clearly thought this through, and with Sam, there is no changing his mind, no change of heart. Funny, how I used to admire his decisiveness. "You want to give them the best day ever?" He doesn't turn to look at me, and I can't tell how intentional it is. "Yeah, like a family trip to Six Flags. They can have all the ice cream and all the turns at those water gun games they want. Then, on the way home—on the drive back—then, we can tell them."

"One last day. The last normal day," I say, processing.

I think back to the Indian restaurant. Surely he chose it because he knew I wouldn't make a scene there, but when confronted, he said it was because he wanted us to have my favorite meal, before he told me. It reminds me of the time right before he and I got married. I spent those weeks wandering around my life, thinking: *This is the last time I'll fill my tax forms out as an individual. This is the last time I will take the train/make a sandwich/do the laundry as a single woman.* I was so sure. I remember asking Sam if he did this, too, and was surprised to hear that the thought had never crossed his mind. The way I'm always writing endings.

It occurs to me that Sam is actually quite controlling in this, not unlike his mother. He wants not only to script but also to cast and to direct the ending: to actualize the scene the way he saw it playing out. (The apple doesn't fall far from the proverbial tree.)

The best day ever. I think this is the dumbest idea ever. I say, "This is the dumbest idea ever." He laughs. Then he realizes I'm serious.

Memory is a funny thing, the way it distorts. If a heart is like a home, then memory is like a fun house. You never know how the mirrors will tilt. Bad memories have a way of casting a film over everything. Bad memories are greedy. They lay claim to a place.

"I don't want to go to Six Flags. I don't want to be the one to ruin Six Flags for them," I say. In this moment, I can't help but imagine my own death: Sam taking the kids on the parachute drop, then telling them that I've died while in line for the Tornado. The mid-ride photo would show their wet faces, but you wouldn't be able to tell if it was the tears or simply part of the amusement park experience. Sam doesn't say anything, just perches on the arm of the couch, the higher ground.

Part of me wants to yell; to throw delicate, breakable things just to hear them shatter and to pointedly not clean them up. I survey my surroundings, looking for a vase or a cup I wouldn't miss terribly. *The last time I drank out of this mug.*

But the mother part of me knows that sound travels in this house. There's a very quiet sound coming from upstairs, the hesitant creak of the door—the sound of curiosity. I don't want to wake the kids, don't want to pull them from their dreams sooner than I need to.

We let the conversation drop, and when I get to our bedroom, I'm not tired at all. I'm energized, actually. Pacing-mad. I circle the room like a plane that can't land. Darlene is probably asleep at this hour, I think, so what do I do with all this inertia? It takes me a little while to figure it out: the perfect small revenge. Sam is somewhat meticulous about his socks. I open the top drawer of his dresser and separate each one from its mate. Mix the argyle pattern with the stripes. Slip a Taco Tuesday one between the solid black pair that is reserved for very important business meetings and funerals. I feel deranged but also good. It'll be moderately disorienting, maybe, but he probably won't say anything. It would be an insane thing to accuse me of doing. And what did you expect? This is what you get with your socks in two places, anyway.

After I'm finished with my little comeuppance, I pull the comforter off the bed. Then the pillows. I make my nest on the floor, curled up on my side of the bed—the side closest to the wall. For all the nights until he goes for real, I don't sleep in the bed, either.

For all the reasons to hate Sam, there were their opposites. When I can't sleep, sometimes I think of that list. Tonight, I think of this thing that Sam used to do earlier in our relationship, when we weren't so new but also definitely weren't so set, so settled.

When we were lying in bed, usually in the humid moments after sex or in the squishy moments between dreaming, he would tell me stories about our life. Sometimes they were things that never happened. Sometimes they were things that could happen, someday. In my shabby little apartment, with the good afternoon light, he would tell me about the house we were going to have: the square footage and the yard space, the name of the latticework on the hardwood floors. Pocket doors. Window boxes with—and here he'd pause and prompt me to fill in the blanks. Basil and mint in the window boxes. Tiger lilies (my favorite) in the front garden. A suncatcher in the kitchen above the sink. Here and there, in this dream house, the splashes of my choice.

He would tell me stories about our love, goofy things. "Do you remember," he would begin dreamily, "when we lived inside that whale?" The first time, I laughed. "That's Pinocchio and his *father*," I clarified, but Sam shook his head. "No, it was us." I found this very charming. Maybe still do. Poetic, and imaginative—a way of telling me that our love existed beyond this sliver of the story. And he said it with the brazen conviction of a young boy you didn't want to shatter.

Half thoughts, half dreams, his tongue loose with an otherworldly lucidity. "When I was Saturn," he said, after we got engaged, "and I gave you all my rings." Another: "I was the sky, and you were the soil. And all the weather—the rays of sun, the rain— were my attempt to meet you."

Now all my days were a flatline gray. But I was the first person, the first captive audience. Before the kids' bedtime stories, there was me and Sam in this bed, his boundless imagination lifting us into another life.

*

On the staircase, there are family portraits, because it seems like something happy homes have, at least in the movies. It's important, I think, that it's not just any old hallway, but the staircase in particular: an ascension. Like, if someone were in your house for the first time. Most guests probably stay downstairs, but close friends would be allowed to venture up. It gives the impression of reaching a higher level of intimacy.

In hindsight, it also seems like kind of a cop-out, to display your family in this odd part of the house, an area where you presumably spend the least time. A banishment of sorts. A private family tree.

There's a photo of my mother that I tend to snag on. Her hair is long—longer than I'd ever seen it in our lives together—and she's wearing a letterman jacket and holding a cigarette. The photo was taken from below, so she comes across as a larger-than-life figure, even though in real life she stood at an even five foot three. (Though maybe she was taller in the days of her youth; you know the shrinking that comes with old age.) She was the only one in the family who knew how to operate a camera, which means she took the photo herself. She liked the tangibility of memory. In the stairwell, I used to be struck by how modern she looked. Well, I say *modern* but I think I meant *American*, by which I actually think I meant *white*. The flash lightens; it makes a ghost of you.

These days, I find myself pausing in the middle of the staircase much more. All those photos—stories we had taken for granted—have started to take up more space, to jump out at me. I touch my hands to their faces. Leave fingerprints on the glass.

There's my son Hula-Hooping out in front of the Skylon Tower on our trip to Niagara Falls. This was before our daughter was born. She was about the size of a peach pit, but technically she was there, too. She gets so sulky when she hears about this trip, like she's insulted she wasn't invited. ("Where was I??") I promise her we will do the trip again someday soon, but in the meantime, her brother likes to taunt her with details about the revolving restaurant that I suspect are more borrowed anecdotes from me than actual recollections. ("You can watch the whole city pass by. It *spins* in the *air*! It's super dangerous. And the French fries are really good.")

There's one of my husband as a child that I simply adore. He's sitting on the couch of his childhood home. There are blue and white balloons in the corner, and he's wearing one of those paper cone birthday hats off to the side. He's smiling wide but with his mouth clamped shut ("I had just lost both front teeth—it was embarrassing!"), which honestly makes him look a touch smug and is more or less how he smiles even now, adult front teeth grown in and all. (Even in our wedding photos.) It's disorienting to see him there, so innocent and so recognizable at the same time. It's unbelievable to me that this sweet child could be capable of inflicting such pain.

Of course, there are the obligatory standard snapshots for School Picture Day. For her first one in preschool, my daughter had fretted for weeks over which costume to wear that day. She didn't much like the idea of being stuck inside the frame that way. (She swiped across the glass with her pointer finger when we first had it framed. "It can't change?" she demanded to know.) I have since fashioned a few fun accessories (a crown, an eye patch, a small bird to perch, etc.) out of construction paper that she can carefully tape on when the need to be a different person strikes her. For this reason, her school portrait is located lower down, where she can reach it.

There's an intimate chaos behind every family group shot. Maybe it's the inherent cruelty in the way someone used to have to always be left out. I was always the one holding the camera, in need of proof of this happy life we built. Always the one desperate to make life still.

Even when we remembered to use the self-timer, it was always me framing the shot: looking out at my family with the lens between us. Running to fill whatever space they had left for me.

There's this one photo of the three of them standing by the boathouse in the park. My son must have been nearly my daughter's age, which means she must have basically been a newborn. I had been setting the self-timer but slipped on the grass, wet with dew, in my frenzy to get back to them. The shutter clicked in the second before they fully processed what had happened. They would forever have those smiles plastered on their faces.

*

In the yard, my son is cutting worms in half. It is a cloudless day, but the wrath of a recent rain has driven the worms out of hiding. The knees of Noah's cargo pants are stained with a light layer of mud.

Kneeling is a funny action, I think. There's something religious about it, certainly. It shows an inherent subservience. When my husband proposed, he got down on one knee, as they tell you a good man should. It's important that it's just the one. It doesn't allow the woman to be an object of full worship.

But then there's the other kind of kneeling, born out of curiosity or the need to get closer. If there is a god up there in that cloudless sky, could he look like my son, back bent, knees in the mud, inspecting his domain?

My son is surprisingly good with the knife. My impulse is to take it away from him—I'm not even sure where he got it—but I watch his mesmerizingly careful incisions instead. He tells me that sometimes the worms grow back—then you get *two*. "But not caterpillars," he says gravely. (My son, learning that there are winners and losers in this life.)

I seize the opportunity. I go to him, muddy my pant legs, too. I say, "You might know your dad and I have not been getting along very well lately." I think of their bedroom door creaking open when Sam and I were talking about Six Flags the other night. I say, "It's just that we're not as close as we used to be." It's not an outright lie; it's the truth with shadows. I don't want to turn their father into the villain—not while they're the audience, at least. My son doesn't look up from the worms. He exhales like he's bored of this conversation already. To be fair, I guess he lives in the house with it all, too. For a second, I wonder if everyone knew but me. If there was ever a woman's voice on their dad's phone interrupting bedtime stories. If he ever told them a story that hinged on moral relativity, second chances, and finding a great love to assuage his guilt—if that was his subtle reveal to them, so they would feel like they had heard this story before and survived it. And then I panic about how Noah's going to describe this scene to a therapist, years later. I even (very briefly) wish I were at Six Flags.

I circle around it for a little while, but then I know I have to land eventually:

"Your dad and I are splitting up."

There. There it is. I'd never heard it phrased like that before. Before today, it was "Are we splitting up?" and "I guess we're splitting up," and even "He's leaving me" (to Darlene). Once, it was "My husband and I are splitting up" (to an awfully sympathetic pharmacist). But this new one is my least favorite phrasing of them all.

He doesn't look up. That's fine by me. I feel the clichés coming— the "This doesn't change how much we love you" line and the "We're still a family" lie. But kids are smart, you know. Instead, I tell him we will be like a regenerative worm. We can be two full families, functioning and everything. He doesn't torture the worms anymore after this.

Also, I look this up, and it's not even true! The head, if the body is cut properly, can grow a new tail, but the tail end is unable to generate the vital parts: head, heart.

*

People are so funny when they're mad at you but they won't come out and say it. They speak in one-word answers, for example, or they walk just a *little* bit ahead of you even if you're going the same way.

I can tell that Sam is mad at me but is trying to conceal it. When he's at the house, he tiptoes around like he's a guest, but he won't make eye contact with me. It's all very passive-aggressively polite. He closes cabinet drawers just slightly harder than is necessary, and I know it's because I told Noah about the separation without him present. Without his permission. But he's also aware that he's ultimately in the wrong here, and Sam avoids battles if he knows he's going to lose them.

"He's used to thinking of you as the victim," Darlene says when I try to explain this weird tension in my house. "He doesn't like that you took control of this story."

*

Darlene and I meet up for a quick bite at this ramen place called Names that used to be a breakfast place. (It used to be called something else, back when they served breakfast, but they were being sued by a large chain for trademark infringement, which was tenuous at best. The new name: an exasperated throwing up of hands I could relate to.)

"Any update from the doctors?" Darlene checks in. It's our new way of greeting one another, apparently. I shake my head, and we try our best to move on. She hands me her phone because she's been debating meeting up with some women from the apps and wants me to weigh in.

It's funny how we give physical sensations to abstract concepts: the undeniable heft of a decision (weigh in, tip the scales), passion or rage as something hot, while humor can be dry as gin but not wet.

If Darlene has just started seeing someone, she'll enter her name into her contacts list, but every time this woman does something to piss Darlene off, she'll delete a letter, like a game of Hangman in reverse. Once the poor girl is all out of letters, she's also out of chances.

"This is unfair," I say to Darlene, who has a relatively long first name. "You'd have *seven* chances by your own standards," I say. "Think about all the great girls with short names you're missing out on! A Lily would have only four chances," I point out. "What about Eve? The *first woman*?"

"Three strikes and you're out!" she says, slurping up her ramen.

Talking to Darlene about dating on the precipice of my own singlehood makes me more afraid of the prospect of getting back out there, someday. It seems like the pool is no better than it was when we were in college. She shows me the dating apps: the way you can now include voice memos or have AI help you write your profile. The way you can filter by political affiliation or religion or height or astrology sign. All these safeguards in place to keep you from falling in love with the wrong person.

I let myself imagine, for a minute, the way it might feel to try to start again. To download one of these apps and to comb through my phone for lovable photographs of myself. I scroll through my phone's camera roll and realize that all the photos I have are of my children. I think of what my profile page would say: Mother. Divorcée. Scorpio.

This exercise is painful for so many reasons. I can't believe my husband had the energy to do this all over again. To learn allergies and favorites, worries and dreams. (I feel like I do this with the kids every day as it is.) To have to tell your own life story again; to reconstruct the narrative for someone who wasn't there; to excavate your past and mine it for gold that you can hand to some stranger; to hang your hopes on someone new; to reference something specific and to realize that the person you're talking to is not the person who was laughing beside you when it all went down—does that ever happen? Does he ever look at Maggie and think of some inside joke, something that existed just between us? It all feels too much to even approach. Maybe this is why Darlene reduces everyone to their name to start. Otherwise, it all just gets too big.

And then, for me, there is also the very real possibility that there is no time to start over. I'm not sure which scares me more: the work of making myself and my life desirable again or the fact that it could just stop—that there might just be meeting new doctors and surgeons and physical therapists and estate lawyers before there is time to let any love in.

*

The body is a playground for disease. The actual playground loosely resembles a body to me now. My kids wriggle their way out of the covered slide. A rebirth. The way they look inside the coil of metal rings—as though inside a rib cage.

They'll be teenagers in a few years. All the heightened emotion, all the hormones. I don't envy them. They say the intensity of your emotions dulls with age, but the complexity of emotions increases—more mixed feelings, things that are bittersweet.

For me, this has largely proven to be true, with the exception of one primal thing: fear. My fear has only grown.

Fear for other people is the absolute worst because there are not one but *two* variable factors in the situation: the thing you're afraid of and the beloved you feel fear for. It is the ultimate loss of control.

I wear my fear on my sleeve. I wear it on my face in the form of little crow's feet creeping up around my eyes. (I thought Asians didn't raisin! A myth of its own.)

And it's different from worry. Worrying feels passive. Worry lives in the mind. It's a mental exercise of things that *could* go wrong. But fear comes alive in the body. Having kids puts me back in my body this way.

How would you measure fear? In heartbeats per minute, in milliliters of sweat. How to describe that cold, icy feeling that spreads through the chest and into the limbs, as though the body were trying to sedate itself?

My fears have grown more specific with time. When I was a kid, like my kids, I was afraid of the dark and what might be inside it. I feared the unknown. Now my fear draws inspiration from headlines: horror stories about strangers on subway platforms with bad tempers and angry, disappointed white men meandering in the halls of schools with guns. I fear rabid opossums and the unlucky timing of cars without rearview cameras backing up just as a ball flies into the street. I fear buildings collapsing and escalators malfunctioning and splinters hidden in charming wooden playgrounds that go unnoticed. I fear Noah's arm bent backward from a tree-climbing endeavor gone wrong. Lily chipping her tooth on something sweet. When we're out at Oyster Bay, I fear the rapid push and pull of the waves with no regard for what gets swept in. Blink—and they'll be gone. I fear pedophiles and rapists and racists, kidnappers. Electric sockets, plastic bags. I fear ear infections.

When both children were born, I feared the little soft spot on their skull—the one people warn you about. I feared blankets pulled too high and ungated staircases. Kitchen cabinets. Corners, ledges. Stovetops. The way the color of Tide pods or plastic beads might be attractive to a child. (Never mind the fact that we had neither in the house.) I feared accidentally killing them all the time. For the first year especially, I feared myself: my own inabilities as a mother.

At the science museum, there's a computer game about survival of the fittest. You are in the middle of the food chain. You are a triangle. The circles are prey. The squares are predators. You can give your triangle points toward certain traits: speed, strength, intelligence, courage, fear. Everyone stocks up on the first four. The brave ones never make it out alive. From this, we learn: your fear will save you.

It's the opposite of what we teach them in telling stories of valor, tales of heroes pulling swords from stones and journeying on the high seas in storms.

"Buck up!" Sam will sometimes say to them, especially to Noah. "Don't be afraid."

*

When the doctor does call, I'm alone in the house. This is a small mercy. It's morning. I had been crossing over from the living room to the kitchen to see what I might scrounge up for dinner; I had been debating making a tofu stir-fry; I had been trying to remember if we were all out of rice. When my phone lights up, I go to the corner of the room before I accept the call. It's a funny instinct, to step aside in your own home, even when you're by yourself.

"Good morning!" the doctor says, when I finally answer. "It's Dr. Wei. Is now a good time?" The question almost makes me laugh; there is no such thing as a good time. There are always dishes to wash and floors to sweep and toilets to scrub, laundry to fold. Even during the early minutes of this call, as I stand at the precipice between healthy and capital-*S* Sick, my attention is trained on the cereal crumbs sprayed across the table. Instead of sweeping them up in one fell swoop, I pick them up one by one, pressing down on each textured crumb so that it would stick to my fingertip.

Dr. Wei tells me that she got the results from my biopsy—and the pause she places in between this sentence and the next says it all. Inside this pause, a life sentence. Inside this pause, a black hole that feels like it's eating everything. Inside this pause, the truth about me.

"There's no easy way to say this, so I'm just going to tell it to you straight," Dr. Wei says. "The biopsy indicated that cancer cells are present in your right breast. You have breast cancer. *But* the good news is that we caught it early. At this stage, it's treatable."

Honestly, my immediate reaction is more passive than one might expect. On the forums, women admit to sobbing or arguing with the doctor about how that can't be true, fainting or even throwing up, right there in the room. They all had some sort of visceral, physical reaction. I'm slower to process the information, maybe. Or at the very least: I want to be seen as an easier patient. Having worked years of customer service after college, on the other side of the counter, I want to be everyone's favorite customer. "Thank you so much for calling, Dr. Wei," I say, forcing my voice to live in that register at the top of the throat/mouth that conveys bright feminine earnestness.

But of course one of my early thoughts (following *oh crap* and *how many more times do I have to keep going back to the office, then?*) drifts to my daughter, and the poison that I have passed down. The blood in the water. A game of Telephone and the misinformation my body whispered into hers.

Surely some of Sam's genetics have won this fight, right? In *this* way, I want her to be more like Sam. I sit with the confusing push and pull of wanting your kids to be more like the person who hurt you.

*

A few years ago, Noah got really into that annoying parroting thing that kids take a liking to. When his father would come home from work—there was Noah, right at his heel. It was uncanny, really, the way he could adjust his gestures and snap his spine to attention, the formal and proper posture Sam had always upheld. Noah was his perfect shadow.

And I have always been a little envious of the ways our kids grow toward their dad, like he's the sun they might revolve around, and I'm some minor orbiting moon, tumbling through space after them.

"It's a scarcity mindset thing," Darlene says, when I confess this feeling to her. "You're just around more. They take for granted that you'll be around."

Would they love me more if I was a more absent parent? Would they cling to my legs and beg me not to go? I imagine the next couple of months playing out: nights spent away from me; me, in and out of hospital rooms, rushing off to doctors' appointments. Would they love me more this way?

*

Cancer cells start out like any other normal cells. What makes them a danger is the way they mutate, and then the way they refuse to die. A stubborn insistence on survival. "It's that immigrant mentality, encoded in my DNA," I joke to Darlene, who is not laughing.

*

In private moments, I find myself touching the lump like a worry stone, the way you might run your tongue compulsively over a toothache or think about an old lover, to see if it still hurts.

(Once I was mindlessly touching the lump at the Pioneer Market, as a zitty young man was ringing up my purchases. Should I have gotten two limes? Did I remember the yogurt cups for the kids? I only noticed when the methodical sound of the scanner stopped and I looked up to find his eyes on me and my breasts. He offered to help me bring my bags to the car. Who says chivalry is dead?)

Darlene thinks we should give it a name. She has always been better at claiming things that way. At owning them and owning up. Me, no, I left both birth certificates blank when we left the hospital, said I had to mull it over. You never realize how many people you hate until you try to name a child.

My son was called "Loud Baby" for the first week or so of his young life. For our daughter, I tried a different tactic: a new name for every hour. A trial period, to see which she fit best. In her early days, she was Sandra, Anne. She wore Haley and Ryan well enough. She napped through Colette. She cried inconsolably when she was Nora. She spit up a little as Vanessa. (In the end, my husband was the one to pick the names of both of our kids.) Meanwhile Darlene had her corgi's name picked out before her application was approved. When we first read Harry Potter with my oldest, Darlene adamantly refuted the concept of "he who must not be named." She read his name aloud, much to the fear of my children.

We settle on Maggie, after my husband's new lover. Like, *you're a cancer, Maggie.* But also like, *look, I have one, too.*

*

When I call with the results of the biopsy, Darlene is quiet for a second, then goes full steam ahead. She has read the reviews on the oncologist I've been referred to. She's cautiously optimistic. But if I don't like that doctor or that plan, that's okay, she assures me. I'm overwhelmed, not by the information itself but by the care that is nested inside it. "Do you have a pen handy?" she asks. She already has more names written down for a second opinion. I start to think of an affair as a second opinion on my marriage.

*

Of course I think about telling Sam. The part of my brain that once wrote rom-com scenes for me and my crushes has found a new hobby. In quiet moments, I find myself lost in some "fantasy" scenario: playing out all the possible ways this conversation could go. In the projector of my imagination: How would I do it? Would I take him back to that same Indian restaurant? (Keep all our bad memories confined to one space in the city.) Should we give him the Best Day Ever? Take him to Six Flags? Would I even have the guts to tell him out loud? I could barely get the sentence out. Terrible words come in threes.

I practice saying them out loud: I have cancer. I have cancer. I have cancer. I write the words down, as though that would help me internalize them, like a naughty student forced to fill the blackboard, a repetitive punishment out of mythology. I contemplate the phrase, the way it gives the holder some agency that doesn't exist. Cancer has me, caught in its clutches.

And isn't it strange—not to be able to discuss all this with the person I've been planning my adult life with? *This*, I realize, is the first time that I will not have Sam as a sounding board. Everything is echoey without him.

It's like a room in the house has been torn out. Your favorite room. The roof tiles are down and the studs in the wall are exposed. A big gaping hole in your home. The best room, the one you went to when you sought comfort. The room with the good sunny spot. The room in which you felt most like yourself. The place you felt most held. Most protected. Now a place you can never put your slippers on again.

Sam is the best possible person to get reassurance from because he genuinely believes everything will always be all right. Life has never given him a reason to think otherwise. It could be so easy to fall into his arms and cry, to be enveloped in his assuredness, the sturdy ground I lived on. He would feel the tug of familial responsibility, surely. He would take care of things. He would have to. He would forget all about Maggie, wouldn't he? He would be jolted back to our vows. *In sickness and in health.* He would hear himself say those words like a siren call delivering him back to me at seven o'clock on the dot every evening. He would step inside our front door and change out of his office clothes and into his Sunday sweats. He would turn on *PBS News Hour* and help chop the onions and he would sit down for dinner across from me, the way he always had. He would tell me how glad he was to see my face. He would dry the dishes after I'd washed them. He would make sure the kids brushed their teeth, and he would let me tell the stories. He would leave momentarily to take out the trash, but he would always come home.

In a way, this could be the worst thing that has ever happened to him. There's a twisted part of my ego that wants to bring that hammer down—that wants to be someone consequential, capable of pulling the rug out from under him for once, for the first time in his polished life. Maybe I want him to feel like this was his fault, somehow. Maybe I want him to feel like a bad person, the worst person in the world.

But the better part of me—the part that wins out—feels like this vulnerability isn't his business anymore. I almost don't want to tell him, ever. It feels like an intimacy he no longer deserves. Or maybe I just don't want him to confuse the indulgent frenzy of panic with love.

*

"Do you still love him?" Darlene asks me, over the phone. It's late. I'm sitting in the hallway, outside the kids' bedroom, picking at the carpet and listening for the settled sounds of sleep. Downstairs, Sam is watching the baseball game on his laptop, with headphones on. I see what he's doing with the time he has left here. He's trying to take up as little space and sound and TV time as possible, to make himself so small he nearly disappears. Normally, Sam solidly occupies a place. He's boisterous. You know when he's in the room; he's got his own gravitational pull and everything moves toward it. "Golden retriever energy," Darlene said, when they first met. It's odd, to see the golden retriever in him retreat with his tail between his legs. His very own theater of remorse, and it's working on me all the same.

I nod. "Are you nodding?" she asks.

Sam is just so *Sam*. You can't help but love him. I think of the list Darlene made me make about my least favorite things. I consider more counterweights:

Before we lived together, he would see me off on the train platform and fake like he was going to race the train car, keeping up with my window as long as he could.

On the rare days that he beats me home—if I've gone out with Darlene for a drink or something—he'll leave Post-it notes on the front door welcoming me home.

When Noah was nervous about performing in the elementary school talent show, he stood up in the audience (front row) and did the dance with him.

He loves weird road trip attractions—the Biggest, the Smallest, the Heaviest—and is all too willing to drive two hours out of the way to find them.

The red Henley shirt he sleeps in every night.

He calls his grandmother, religiously, every Sunday on the way back from the grocery store.

The way he bunny-ears his shoelaces.

I think of the night we first met. I was checking on my pizza; he was ordering an IPA. "Would it be *cheesy* to say that our orders would go well together?" he asked, by way of a pickup line. A dumb thing to say, really, because pizza goes with everything. But the pun was just so bad and I needed a laugh, and that, as they say, was that. Even when gorgeous girls eyed him with an intensity that could be felt from across the bar, even when his friends came to close out their tabs and wrangle him to the second location, he didn't budge. He stood next to me all night, and I felt like I had won something.

*

I'm told I have options. The specialist lays all two of them out for me:

I can get a breast-conserving surgery, which would (as the name implies) allow me to keep the majority of my breasts. I would likely also need radiation. I learn radiation is different from chemo. "You get to keep your hair!" the doctor said to me, as though this was the most important thing. I'll have to come back every day for a few weeks. "Except on weekends," she tells me. "Why weekends?" I ask. "Because we're closed," she says, shrugging.

I can get a preventive double mastectomy: take both girls out in one go and most likely have much less to worry about.

I'm told I should also meet with a plastic surgeon, just for a consultation. The specialist hands me a business card, and it feels like maybe a pyramid scheme or, at the very least, the kind of chain mail we got in the early aughts that lorded bad luck over you if you didn't pass it on. (In this scenario, I'm the bad luck.)

*

My mother never wanted me to take the BRCA exam, the one that can tell you how likely it is that you've inherited this mutation from your mother. She said it was because she was afraid I might have to disclose the results on some insurance form someday, which would complicate my future coverage. Preexisting conditions and whatnot.

In hindsight, I think she was afraid of the certainty of blame. Someone to point the finger at. Maybe she felt that ignorance was bliss, like knowing was opening the door to something bad. That it was unlucky to poke at the beast. Some superstition in it. Like if you say its name, it will appear.

*

The plastic surgeon's office is in an inconvenient location, accessible only by a train line I don't live near. It's one of those offices with a wall of fake plants and a therapy dog named Luna that greets you at the glass door. Everyone who works here is attractive. Scrubs somehow look cute on these people. The receptionist has me fill out the cursory forms that are the same everywhere, except there is a little section at the bottom that asks if you have a preferred Spotify playlist that you'd like them to put on in your room.

The plastic surgeon is a very enthusiastic man who teases that he's done work on a few B-list celebrities but won't tell me who. "Doctor-patient confidentiality," he cites.

Marriage meant I hadn't shown my breasts to strangers in a long time, but motherhood sort of meant the opposite, what with the unpredictability of feeding. I let the little pink robe flap open and am honestly unfazed by this part of the process. It's the small talk that I find most awkward about these moments.

"How did you get into plastic surgery?" I ask him, my go-to question in situations like these, and he tells me that he actually wanted to be a sculptor but knew he couldn't afford a life on that gamble, that plastic surgery was the most hands-on medicine he could imagine, that he got to spend his days making people beautiful.

When I get home, I call Darlene and tell her that if the ceramics thing doesn't pan out, she would probably make a pretty good plastic surgeon. "Who knew beauty could be a type of medicine?" Darlene muses. "I thought that was supposed to be laughter."

We go on about how unbelievable it is that not one but *two* of my doctors wanted to be artists: these glimmers of other lives.

*

My favorite alternate profession is mitigation investigator. A long time ago, I met the spouse of someone at one of Sam's company holiday parties in this specific line of work. She said her job was to work with individuals who have been found guilty of a serious crime. After they'd been convicted by the jury—that was when she stepped in. Her job was to convince twelve strangers to vote for a life sentence instead of the death penalty. To do this, she pulled at all the threads of this person's life, combing through it for anything that might explain away some of the wrong. (Examples of this, she told me, included researching their childhood apartment building to see if it contained lead paint or interviewing their middle school bus driver, someone who had seen the kid every day and could surely convey if they had been malnourished or mistreated in their youth.) Her job was to tell the story of someone's life in order to save it.

Is this what I'm doing now? Playing the story back again in a desperate attempt to understand, to hit upon some key, irreversible detail that I missed the first time around? If I play it slower, will I see it coming this time? Will it hurt any less?

*

Lily once had a Winnie-the-Pooh snow globe bestowed upon her by Sam's parents. She was obsessed with it. She held the Hundred Acre Wood in her hands. She carried it with her everywhere. One day, she and I were playing shop. (Isn't it funny—the way kids want to mimic our mundanity?) She was ringing me up with her plastic cash register, and somewhere in between her hands and mine, we fumbled and lost that little world.

The look on her face that day—that shattering disappointment—that's the face she has on when Sam and I sit her down and tell her about the separation, together.

We sit an awkward distance away from each other on the couch.

As we call her in, I think, *This is the last time she'll see "family" as one cohesive thing. This is the last time she'll lump me into "Mom and Dad."* She'll see us as separate entities now, me on my own without the context, and that terrifies me, too.

Sam is the one to put this awful truth in out-loud words. He hurries it on, like he's afraid I'm going to jump in and steal the show. It's worse than when he told me at the restaurant. At least there, I had samosas. Something to do with my hands. This time, I barely process the words when he says them. They sound far away to me, like I'm underwater. Drowning.

I wish I was holding *The Big Book of Anti-Jokes*, a life raft.

I don't so much hear the words as I do watch them burrow into Lily's face. I don't turn to Sam when he's talking; I keep my eyes trained on our daughter the whole time. I know it's all been said when her face looks like the snow globe has been dropped again. The allegory of the cave, and I'm never facing the right way. Lily cries. The sound of it brings me back into the room.

And it makes me feel very small all of a sudden. It occurs to me how little I can protect her from the hurt of living. Life will always have its jolts, sure, but that was for when they were older. Teenage heartbreak, college rejections, that kind of thing. At this age, the only surprise should be drawing that card in Candy Land that tells you to go back a few steps. Yes, maybe that's what the point of that mean-spirited card is: to prepare you for the shocking things that will set you back later in life. As a parent, I thought it was my job to create the perfect control environment, as best I could.

This is when it really sinks in for me: that I will not always be there when her face looks like this, when she's making this wailing sound. I have an urge to join her, a sad chorus. I had a hard enough time letting them go off to school, letting them be whisked away by their grandparents. But now, for her, there will exist some version of home that I'm not a part of.

*

Doctors are very careful to slip in things like *most likely* and *best chance*, because there are no guarantees.

*

Even when he's packing up his things or taking the kids someplace, even in the middle of this shit storm, there are little moments when I see the Sam I knew. When he says something funny or makes this pensive facial expression I have quietly adored or hums a song we used to dance to. He peeks through the spaces in between the dense forest that has grown between us, shoots through like dappled sunlight.

In moments like these, it's like nothing has happened. No Maggie. No kids even. The way that certain angles of sun and warmth can hit you exactly like they did in your youth; sun that has been untouched by time. Just like he said: he was the sky, and I was the soil, and the weather was his attempt to meet me. This is when the heartbreak hits me hardest. When he reminds me of the people we used to be, when we had so much in front of us. This is when I most want to let him in on things. He transforms back into someone I want to tell my life to.

And then something shifts in the atmosphere, and the moment—that person—is gone.

*

On one of our walks through the park, Darlene turns to me and says, "Did you know breast cancer is the most common type of cancer there is? You're basic, Maggie!"

*

At home, against my better judgment, I google some basic facts. For scale:

310,720. That's how many women were diagnosed with breast cancer last year in the US.

673,989. That's how many people got divorced last year in the US.

3.66 million. That's how many babies were born last year in the US.

120 million. That's how many George Foreman grills have been sold in the US since 1994.

My comparisons remind me of that trip to the science museum with my children, the little signs that compare the weights and sizes of dinosaurs to things we can comprehend. It's a very human instinct: to bring things too big for our understanding down to our level.

Is that what Sam has done? Brought love to scale? Condensed it into something easily comparable to himself, something he could comprehend?

There's a memory that comes back to me, one of my favorites. It was summer then like it will be soon. Muggy and sunny, with everyone shedding layers, the season in which people seem to be most borderless. Most receptive to conversations with strangers—and purchasing things from stoops. Our kids wanted to have a lemonade stand, and Sam was very supportive and enthusiastic about our burgeoning entrepreneurs. This is something I loved about Sam, how excited he always was to begin a project. I've come to understand that there are two types of people: Beginners and Enders. Sam was very much a Beginner, with an unburdened optimism that I cherished being around. Of course, the fact that he loved kicking off new things had another side to it. He seldom finished them.

On that summer day, he got the plastic pitchers from the back of the cupboard and helped the kids squeeze the lemons and mix the sugar in evenly. He pulled a little folding table out from the basement and even made them a sign that read: "FRESH" LEMONADE! ONLY $2!

One of the things I find funniest in this dark little world is misplaced quotation marks. "I'm sorry" if that makes me a grammar snob, but the implication of a sarcastic *fresh* made me double over with laughter, something I could not explain to the kids or to Sam. I laughed, and I was alone in my laughter. It felt lonely.

Actually, Sam went back inside shortly thereafter, which I took to mean I had offended him (I remember apologizing later that night). Looking back now, I see that it was just another example of a thing Sam didn't see through to the end.

But life has a funny way of coming full circle. In stalking Maggie on the internet, I realize that the misplaced quotation marks are just another thing they have in common. Under every mirror selfie post, Maggie writes: *"outfit of the day."* Under every group shot, *"Blessed."*

*

I opt for the breast-conserving surgery, because my oncologist told me that this procedure has a shorter recovery time while still giving me a very good shot. I'm relieved to hear this; I want to save as much of myself as possible. In the days leading up to the surgery, I find myself telling the kids stories from my own life at bedtime. I'm a squirrel, storing nuts for the winter, just in case. They go to brush their teeth, and when they return, there I am: the troll under the bridge, ready with my riddles, asking them to help me make sense of things before they can pass into the land of sleep.

They aren't so much stories as they are small anecdotes: that I broke my arm when I was in the second grade and nearly (unfairly) flunked music because I couldn't play the recorder; that the favorite son of a close family friend used to pour Sprite into my rice when they visited for dinner, so I'd have no choice but to eat it with a straight face or risk embarrassing my mother by complaining about the food ("Don't get any bright ideas," I say, my voice in that particular register of parental warning); that I believed in the protective luck of jade because once, in college, when I rested my wrist on the green of a pool table, a cue ball came out of nowhere and cracked my jade bangle bracelet clean in half. There's no point to these stories, no particular shape or message to hammer home. "Remember when . . . ?" I begin a story that involves the kids, less a question and more a request, a plea. Please remember when.

They protest. "This isn't what we signed up for," they point out. "Tell us a *real* story," they say, as though they came expecting gemstones, and all I had was plain old rocks that I couldn't make shine.

*

The first time I met Sam's family was at Christmas. This is always a great time to meet someone's parents for the first time, because you will not be the focal point, and everyone will be weird and stressed anyway.

Right before dinner, they asked me to take their big family photo in front of the tree. Fair. I was new. No one was sure just how serious Sam and I were yet—not even us. Sam's parents stood like pillars in the center, flanking him on either side. His uncles and aunts and cousins all filtered in, and the little cousins sat on the floor. It was hard to get a shot without them making bunny ears behind one another, much to the dismay of Sam's parents. They shunned the concept of silly sweaters or matching hats, but they all had the same tight-lipped smile. It was the last big family photo they had without me in it.

I specifically remember looking through the viewfinder and thinking how funny it was that I was the one framing this memory. Always the one holding the camera, I felt a little bit outside of the present. It was a form of time travel. To take the photo, you're looking through the lens of some future someone, looking back on this day. You are the record keeper. I remember thinking, *No matter what happens with me and Sam, many years from now, this photo will exist in some leather-bound family album or hung up in some dark stairwell that everyone will walk by every day but never really see again.* There is some secret power in being the one taking the shot.

*

When I was growing up, in my own family, there wasn't much of a model for expressing emotion. Rather, my parents made a clear distinction between inside emotions and outside emotions, like home clothes and street clothes, things you could peel off at the boundary of home. Emotions you could feel publicly included: joy, excitement, gratitude, and maybe surprise. You could get away with boredom or annoyance if you were able to scrub it from your face quickly enough. Inside emotions were the rest of them: anger, sadness, fear.

When my husband first told me about Maggie, I must have cried. At some point. In my memory of how that evening played out, I handled it very well. I did not make a scene. I did not cry, and I did not yell. Most importantly: I did not beg. Maybe this was the exact reason I asked *who* and *where* and *when* but not *why*. There was no way to ask *why* without sounding a little desperate. It wasn't a question I felt I could ask with dignity. Besides, *why* wasn't a question you got to ask if you had not lived a lucky life. People like Sam got to ask *why*. Instead, I was perfect as a statue. My mother would've been very proud of my stoicism.

But even when we returned home, I realize now, I didn't let the facade fall. I didn't break down—not in front of Sam. It was as if he had already become part of the outside to me, like my boundary of home receded a little closer to myself.

But surely I must have cried, sometime after dinner. Sometime in the quiet aloneness of our room without him. I know this because weeks later, I reach my hands into the pocket of an old hoodie that I usually put on when I get home and pull out a wad of dried tissues, disintegrating in the way that told you they held a lot of sadness, once. A physical manifestation, proof of my feeling of loss. You could weigh them. There, that's the exact amount of sad I was. Finally: a way to compare pain.

*

My husband is a deeply religious man when it suits him. He wanted to get married in church, the way that people who were raised with a specific and personal god often do. He was someone who felt above therapy, preferring confession. Well, here's mine: I'm the first to admit that I'm not the best wife.

I'm always conveniently preoccupied when the drain needs to be scooped out.

I don't like breaking down big boxes, and sometimes I try to convince my children to use them to build a fort—that's how lazy I am.

I watch movies—always romantic comedies—when I cook, and I burn the salmon. (It was something he used to find endearing, I think, when *You've Got Mail* or some other romantic comedy I had seen a thousand times would cast sound waves in our kitchen, and I'd get caught up in them, and an unidentifiable meal would blacken on the stove. "It was made with love." That was our little bit about it.)

And I had absolutely no idea that this infidelity was weighing on my husband's heart. They talk about women's intuition and the way a mother always knows. I never suspected a thing.

"It's not your fault. You know that, right?" This is something Darlene says to me, the first night that Sam spends in his new apartment. It's less startling than I expected; his coming and going has started to feel so normal to me. It's not my fault. I know this, and yet . . . How could I not have known? Surely, there were warning signs. When I try to think of how we were together in this past year, these past few months, he comes out a little hazy in my memory.

We used to be people who pushed each other toward big and scary things that would challenge us and be good for careers and character development. Marriage, though, was more of a pull. We pulled the other person closer, into a whirlpool of domesticity, dirty dishes, dirty diapers, dirty laundry, family, in-laws, elaborate Christmas dinners. Family had its own gravity, knotted us into one contained unit. Family is a forest of its own, and I think along the way, we stopped being able to see some of the trees.

*

"I'll tell him after the surgery." This is the promise I make to Darlene, and myself. We're sitting behind Darlene's booth at the pop-up artists' market. It's the kind of spring day that warns you that a hot summer is coming. It forces you to feel your body: the way your sweat runs down your hairline and pools in places and your thighs stick to every seat. It's one of those days when you look at perfectly un-sweaty people wearing blue jeans and wonder where their glands are. You are painfully aware that you are thirsty and gross.

We stack Darlene's ceramics up high in front of us with the hopes that no one will really look at us. We've got a bunch of little ring trays/kitchen sponge holders and dessert plates and a few mugs—just in case the casual customer doesn't feel like picking up an urn today. It's just good business sense.

Roberta is doing a great job of enticing customers to come say hi, then scaring them away with her shrill barks. She's picky about customers, which means we have a bit of downtime to talk.

Initially, the health insurance question was another anvil hanging over my head. I was afraid I might have to ask Sam to stay married to me, just until all the proper procedures had been done. Maggie—the tear and the tether.

But, as it turns out, in some divorce cases, you can stay on your ex-spouse's health insurance for as long as thirty-six months. I'm guessing it has something to do with how long it takes someone at the firm to process the paperwork, but I'm not complaining. The bureaucracy has, for once, worked in my favor.

Besides, "I had cancer" feels much less scary to say than "I have cancer." Those are words I can get my mouth around. The past tense offers protection, a clean sliding door of separation.

*

When I'm not busy writing lists about Sam, I have a list of things I have grown to hate about doctors' offices:

I hate the little boxes on all the forms. The way you have to fit every severed letter individually. It rids you of any notion of connectivity. Mentally, it readies you for separation.

I hate the questions on all the forms. The Forms want to know personal things. As in a fairy tale, the Forms will not let me pass until I've answered their twisted questions correctly. The Forms ask invasive questions about my family's medical history. The Forms prompt me for the cause and age of death of all my grandparents. And perhaps more than I hate the Forms' questions, I hate the shame I feel at not knowing the exact answers; the events that they are inquiring about having happened a long time ago, an ocean and a language away.

I hate the little water dispensers with their tiny triangular paper cups. It's never enough water. The paper cones can't stand on their own, so you're forced to drink the water in one go, up by reception; it feels like you've been called to the front of the class. And then it feels wasteful to throw the "cup" out after just one use. I usually take it back to my seat with me for no reason at all. I suck the water out of it, and then I fold it in half and stick it in some useless front pocket of my purse.

I hate the outdated magazines. They're always several months old. In fact, Darlene and I have made a game of stealing them from the waiting rooms. Slowly and systematically, we purge the periodicals. It feels less like theft and more like a public service, really. The worst culprit in the bunch we've seen so far: an *InStyle* from 2000 with Winona Ryder on the cover, boasting "Sexy and Smart Bras for Every Size," an "Inside Look at Seven Stars' Closets," and "50 Ways to Treat Yourself *Right Now.*" Honestly, it maybe says a lot about the kinds of people they expect to become patients—the kinds of people waiting in these rooms, women interested in *Better Homes & Gardens* and *Glamour.* In all my visits here, I've never seen, say, the *Atlantic* or the *New Yorker* in rooms like these. As though maybe *those* readers would be smart enough not to get cancer.

I hate the temperature in these doctors' offices. It's never quite right. The dial is always tilted a little too much on either end.

I hate the clunky old metal scale with the little weight and the big weight that all doctors always insist on flicking across the metal bar for you.

I hate the way doctors always try to make polite conversation. They always want to know what I *do.* When I tell people I'm a mother, their natural next question is always, "How many kids?" or "How old?" or "What are their names?" The conversation glides happily over me and settles on my children.

I hate the word *exam,* the way that it implies my body is always failing.

*

Mothers are optimists. This is what Darlene tells me when I am being the most down on myself. "I can be as cynical as I want," she says, "but *you* brought new life into this world. That requires a kind of faith that things will always work out." My desire to procreate, an exercise in hope. A stubborn insistence.

*

When I became a mother, my brain reorganized itself. All my thoughts became lists, but up until now, they were usually about my children. Short bursts of things I was forgetting, and things I had not done. On repeat like the stock market ticker in Times Square. A carousel of things. And after the to-do lists, there were the dates: doctor's appointments and PTA meetings and bake sales. And after the dates, there were the current likes and dislikes of my children at that particular moment in time.

Lily

No unpeeled grapes

Yes jelly on crackers

No peas

Yes peanut butter

Noah

Yes bologna sandwiches

No crusts

Yes hot Cheetos

No lunch-box notes

*

When a baby is born, there is so much agony around the name. Some people make a lot of money compiling book-length lists of them every year, which we got several of as gifts from my husband's extended family. I tried to read this as generosity and not a reflection of their lack of trust in us to pick a good (Western) name. Every time a new one would come gift-wrapped in the mail, we'd flip through it exactly once before adding it to the pile we were using to prop open the bad bathroom window.

Sure, we mocked them, but privately I sort of liked that the authority of names went through a cycle of change every year, like the dictionary or the DSM. It was something that could be amended, or added to.

Yes, there's a whole industry based on the anxiety prospective parents have about picking the wrong name, but I feel we don't prepare nearly as much for the fact that our own way of calling ourselves will change.

Before the kids were born, my husband and I had a few cute pet names for one another. There were the standards (honey, babe; you know the drill) and the more customized (Shark, Little Lion Man; don't try to understand it).

Right before the kids were born, we got two new ones: Mom and Dad. In Lamaze class, in the weeks leading up to the first birth, we practiced. In the mirror, alone, I practiced. Mom. Mom. Mom.

Not *someone's* mom—which is a role, a new relationship—but a total shift in identity, the implication that you morph into this other thing. Mom. It becomes the call to which you must respond most often. And how odd it feels to suddenly go by a name you had used for someone else, like donning an old overcoat worn by every woman you know and hoping it somehow fits you, too.

*

Sometimes I find myself wondering how Sam and Maggie say *I love you*. The way a couple develops their own language. Do they say *babe* when they mean it and *dear* when they don't? Does he tell her—as he told me—that he loves her "as deep as the sea"? Or are they still voyagers, finding new ways to land on *I love you*?

*

When I tell Darlene that I want to read some books about single parenting/mothering through a divorce/mourning a marriage/starting over, she does not accompany me to our neighborhood bookstore. No, that's something that a good friend would do. A good friend would help you research the titles you might be interested in and help you decide which of the two covers is the least pathetic-looking in the store. What Darlene does is something that only a very best friend would think of, which is to take me to the next-closest Barnes & Noble. "We'll never see these people again," she tells me, as we glide on in through the automatic doors. She reminds me of the time I was considering a career pivot, when I was debating life as a stay-at-home mother, and I had purchased *What Color Is My Parachute?* from our friends at the bookstore. "You got questions for weeks after!" she says.

At the Barnes & Noble, we are anonymous. At the Barnes & Noble, nobody cares about us. It's the kind of place where you can be left on your own for hours. We plant ourselves on the mildewy carpet of self-help.

Sam has been moving out very slowly. I can't decide how I feel about it. It makes it easier to think he'll come home if his running shoes are still on the rack—but when one day they no longer sit beside your strappy special-occasion sandals, you can't help but wonder where he's run off to now.

There are some things that live in a messy gray area: nice kitchen appliances that we got as wedding presents, arts-and-crafts projects by the kids. Once I reached for a wooden spoon that we won as a couple from a chili-making competition between friends—and it was in a slightly different place. A few instances like this—that's how I know it's something Sam debated taking, probably even packed away, before ultimately deciding to leave it behind.

Every day is like a small vanishing act. Ta-da! I never thought I'd miss the sight of his razor perched on the toilet tank, just so. The little hairs in the sink that he used to leave every morning to accomplish that clean-shave look—gone. Now my sink is always clean, and my kids are always asking why their dad isn't home at night to tuck them into bed and tell them a story. We've explained it to them, of course, time and time again. They'll nod, and they'll say, "Okay," in small voices when we ask if they understand, but the truth is words like *separation* and *divorce* and *moving out* are hollow when you're young like that. At Noah's and Lily's ages, they are just a jumble of letters with no pain nestled inside them yet. Every day, I watch the reality hit a little harder. I watch them pack a little more disappointment into those words.

What I have found is that most of these self-help books will stress consistency as the key. It's best to establish a new baseline of normal as quickly as possible, and to let your children feel like they have some choice in the small things: the color of their room, for instance.

At the start, we will avoid splitting their stuff in two as much as possible. We will not force them to choose which toys fall on which side of the battleground. It's decided that for the time being, they (and all their stuff) will stay with me at the house. My husband will get new things for his new life with them, so it feels less like a fracture and more like an added bonus. Less like something is being taken away, and more like they'll have an excess: of home, of love. All that bullshit we tell ourselves.

*

One of the things that has to be determined when a tumor is discovered is how far it's gone. Has it embedded itself in the tissue? The fact that the body has tissue, built in—the body was born ready to absorb sadness.

The fact that in this world, there's something called HER2. It stands for human epidermal growth factor receptor 2. It's a gene that can play a role in the development of breast cancer. HER2 was apparently always there. She's encoded. You can get the surgery, but it doesn't remove HER2.

*

The day I meet my breast surgeon for the first time, a woman comes up to me in the waiting room. I feel like I've seen her around before, maybe at Dr. Wei's, or in some other horrible waiting room, or in an elevator going down. Sometimes it feels like a very small world. There are those walls—closing in. Today, she wears a thin red Old Navy cardigan. She introduces herself as Linda. In the waiting room, we learn each other's first names only—in the same way that neighbors do when they encounter one another at Starbucks. The attending nurse reads the next name off the clipboard; they are summoned, and then they disappear.

Linda sits down next to me. She's quiet for a minute. And then she tells me that she would recommend letters.

"Letters?"

"For your kids. Just in case."

She tells me that she has written birthday cards for every year till her daughter turns twenty-one. (She's ten now.)

"What do you put in there?" I ask timidly.

"Oh, you know. That I'm proud of her, that I love her. That I hope she's happy. Plus, fifty bucks."

On the way home, I stop at a stationery store. I go to the birthday card aisle, as instructed, and I try to imagine what it is that my kids might want to see in five, ten, fifteen years. A pink-frosted birthday cake? A *T. rex* with a little hat? Two porcupines eating cupcakes? I leave without buying anything.

I don't know if I can picture my kids as anything other than the ages that they are. What will they be like in two years or as teenagers? Some mothers in the PTA claim that they can see it. They *know* that their son will be a gallery-worthy photographer, that their daughter has a knack for entrepreneurship. But I don't even want to try; I like the surprise of it. I want to meet them new every day. When they come home from school—telling me about some new thing they love, or revealing a vitriol or consideration or caution

I have never seen in them before—I resist the urge to shake their hand, say nice to meet you.

But the idea of leaving something "just in case" sticks in my mind. It reminds me of that trend of getting your kids an email address when they're born and sending them photos and memories, the password to come on their eighteenth birthday.

(We never did that.)

(I can't help but wonder if Maggie would be the kind of mother who does something sentimental like that.)

Instead of letters, I start writing down all the lists in my mind, hoping someone else might carry them if I can't.

Lists with information like:

The trash collection comes on Wednesdays and Sundays.

The smoke detector is finicky, so if you're frying eggplant (not a favorite for Lily right now anyway), it's best to take the apparatus down. Use canola oil. Olive oil has a notoriously low smoke point.

Don't tell anyone your mother's maiden name.

Remember your social security numbers. Commit them to the prison of your memory. Know them by heart. (A funny phrase—implies that memory lives more deeply in the heart than in the mind.)

Replace the Brita filter every ~three months.

Seltzer and Dawn dish soap get out tricky stains.

Save the pasta water. Just in case the recipe calls for it later.

*

When I tell Darlene I've started to develop a compulsion with the lists, she thinks I mean a bucket list. Ten Wonders of the World to See Before You Die, that kind of thing. But at a young age, I learned the danger of having specific wants: how easily disappointment can creep in there and envelop the whole dream. Instead, I lived my life casting a wide net. I never said, for example, *I want to travel to Florence, Italy.* Instead, I told myself I wanted to travel, full stop. That way, anything could count. Traveling to see Sam's parents. Traveling to Philly to chaperone a school field trip to see the Liberty Bell. All this was part of what I wanted. I wished for happiness and good friends and real love. And for a little while there, I had it all.

When Sam and I met, I had been overwhelmed by the breadth of his travel stories. Most people I knew had one place. When we were kids, there were the lucky ones who had some other faraway land to return to for the summer. They went away year after year, their families unable to resist a siren call in another tongue. They came back in September with treats for close friends from China and Malaysia and India. I accepted my trinkets gratefully, but every time I looked at them, I envied these friends.

In college, I'd maybe know people by the city they studied in during their semester abroad. I hung postcards from Paris and Istanbul and Tokyo on my wall and stared at them when I was daydreaming, as though through a window into a world I couldn't touch.

But, still, one place per person. That was the economic bracket I was familiar with.

But Sam—whose parents had houses in several states plus "regular" spots in London and Berlin—couldn't be pinned down by one specific place. He had been everywhere. The world was his, and he wasn't beholden to any particular notion of home.

I never learned to drive, which meant I was mostly at the mercy of other people, but happily so. I was always content to sit in the passenger seat. Even when the world was just a miles-paid plane ride away for me, too, I was always content to sit and sip Starbucks coffee out of a firm paper cup and let someone else take me away.

*

My children don't know my real name. Not in a cool spy way (which would impress them), but in the way that many of us have had to scrub ourselves down to the bone for survival. In the way where I was gifted a Chinese name and had it stripped away in kindergarten, when I was little older than my daughter is now. Our teacher—a woman whom I won't give the courtesy of a name to— had pulled me aside after school in the first week and told me that I needed to pick a new name.

"A new name?" I asked.

"An American name."

So I closed my eyes and pointed to a page in the library after school. The way the Dadaists named their art. The butter knife in the book. My real name lived and died in the mouth of my own mother.

Sometimes I dream about how different my life would be under the shelter of another name. Did I choose correctly? Could my life have happened to someone else? Shakespeare said a rose by any other word would smell as sweet. Would we echo it with reverence if a man named Bob had written it instead? For some, names are just flaccid balloon skins, waiting to be filled with the air of meaning. But the rest of us know the weight of them.

*

Somewhere in all of this, my son learns about the moon trees. They're trees grown from seeds that were flown to the moon on Apollo 14. They were actually almost lost when the canister split open upon the astronauts' return to Earth. The majority of them germinated normally, but then they were—for whatever reason—largely forgotten about, left to root and grow and reach for the sun in obscurity. So the story goes: twenty years later, a schoolteacher in Indiana found a plaque on a tree in the schoolyard that read: MOON TREE. And now a NASA scientist is trying to track them all down.

"What's so special about the moon trees?" I ask my son. "Do they glow in the dark or something?"

He shakes his head. "Nothing's special about their appearance." He says this like he thinks it's the coolest thing in the world. "Most of them are sycamores. You wouldn't even know. You wouldn't even know what they went through! You have to know where to look."

*

A tumor, a seed.

*

Summer has always seemed to me the season in which our bodies make their presence most known to us. The swamp of sweat cinched by the elastic of my bralette. Our skin, exposed, in turn exposes our porousness to the world: the vulnerability to mosquito bites and the sun, and though my husband suffers from both, I myself don't mind. In the summer, we can mark the time passing by the amount of daylight our bodies soak in. Our kids always look even more like mine in the summer.

In our final PTA meeting of the school year, all the parents are bragging about their fabulous summer plans: trips to Madrid; Costa Rica; science camp; magic camp; space camp; a stint in Switzerland to visit the grandparents; middle school prep classes; a cousin's wedding in Greece; a family-friendly writing retreat somewhere upstate; Girl Scouts; zip-lining; a private piano tutor; French lessons culminating in a trip to Paris, as though language was not its own reward.

For my family, I have planned nothing. I can't fathom the future from where I'm sitting. I can't picture anything better than long stretches of time with my kids in the house, building forts and playing in the backyard and maybe being welcomed into their make-believe worlds.

To the other parents, I say, "Sam's parents have a place out on Oyster Bay, so we'll be there for a while, by the beach."

*

School's out, and the looser lines of days make the children restless. "Tell us a story of adventure," Noah requests one soupy, humid night. "A new one."

So I pull out a story I haven't heard since my mother told it to me when I was their age. It's one of my favorites:

There was once a scholar who went for a walk in the woods and got lost. It started to rain, and he could not find his way back. He stumbled upon a shrine, a kind of shelter. Inside, there was a painting of a goddess: the most beautiful woman the scholar had ever seen. He was so moved by her beauty that he composed a poem and scrawled it on the wall of the shrine. Then, exhausted from his journey, he fell asleep for the night.

While he was sleeping, the goddess herself emerged from the painting. She read the scholar's poem, and she too was moved. When he awoke, they fell in love. They spent many (mostly) happy years together. And then they even had a child: a baby boy.

After their son was born, the goddess was called back to the heavens. Her two brothers (not to mention the other gods) were displeased with her. Love between a god and a mortal was strictly forbidden. As punishment, one of her brothers banished her to a cave in the far reaches of heaven. She was never to return to earth— never to see her family again.

"Brothers!" Lily squeals.

Meanwhile, the scholar was left heartbroken and with a child he was ill-equipped to care for. As he debated his next move, he went for a walk in the woods with his newborn son in tow. Suddenly, the woods opened up into a clearing: a field, where they met a kind farmer who took pity on their situation, having just fathered a son himself. The farmer proposed a deal: the scholar could work on the farm. His wife would provide milk to the motherless boy. They could raise their sons as brothers. In exchange, the scholar could teach the farmer's son to read.

"To read?" my kids ask.

"A privilege and a power that not everyone has," I tell them, eyeing Noah's unpacked workbooks for the summer.

The farmer wanted his son to get educated, to achieve a higher station in life. But the farmer could not conjure meaning from the shapes on the page the way he could the marks of the soil and the language of the crops. This deal turned out to be one of the best things that ever happened for both families. The boys grew as brothers. For many years, they were all (mostly) happy.

And then one year, the crops were not growing as they should have. In fact, they were dying. Inexplicably. The weather was bad. Something was happening.

The scholar started to hear, after all these years, his beloved goddess speaking to him. She said, "The crops are dying because I am imprisoned here in heaven." She said, "It's only going to get worse." She said, "You have to come and save me."

Noah, employing logic, says, "But she's a goddess! How could this human possibly save her if she can't break out by herself?"

"Yeah!" Lily chimes in.

"Great point!" I tell them. They're already ahead of the story. Something that was very commonly known and accepted was that mortals, try as they might, could not traverse the heavens. It was an irrevocable fact.

However, because the scholar's son was also half god, he stood a chance. By this point, the son was of hero age. "How old?" Noah wants to know. "Seventeen," I say. They're satisfied by this answer; that feels adult enough.

The demigod son would go to the heavens and rescue his mother. His whole-human brother volunteered to accompany him, despite the dangers that were sure to lie ahead. He didn't want his brother to go alone.

So they set off, and the two faced many trials on their way. One caused the death of the farmer's poor son. "Brothers," Lily says quietly, suddenly taken with the concept.

Mourning the loss of his brother but still forced to go on, our demigod eventually found the cave where his mother was imprisoned. To his shock, there were many gods locked in a giant cage there. (As it turns out, the one god brother was on kind of a power trip.)

"Brothers!" Lily says again, accusingly.

Instead of a lock, there was a blank piece of paper.

"No way," Noah says. "That doesn't make any sense. Couldn't the gods just rip that up?"

The piece of paper could only be broken when the blood of a mortal was spilled over it. The logic here being that no mere mortal could make it this far. Our demigod, of course, was both.

He pricked the tip of his finger and drew a line of blood across the scroll, freeing the gods. They overthrew the evil brother god, and as a thank-you, they offered their savior one wish. Of course, he wished his brother back to life. His mother, the goddess, also requested a wish: to be made mortal so that she might live out the rest of her days on earth with her family. Her wish was granted. And they lived many (mostly) happy years together.

Tonight, I feel like a hit. The kids loved this story, the way I hoped they would. I make a mental note to tell it again and again, enough times that they might commit it to memory. There is so much to unpack here! The power of language. The power of being both. They are so enthralled in the narrative that they don't seem to see themselves as our half-blood hero; I just hope they remember this story later, if ever it's helpful to them. The mother needing to lose her godliness to be with her family. The fact of the lock as an empty scroll; the key being your ability to spill your own blood over the page (a kind of storytelling).

*

June, and the bugs are out. Or in, rather. That's the problem. My daughter shrieks at every spider she encounters, and because she's small and observant and has nothing better to do until school starts up again, she finds them with some frequency.

But of course, my son *loves* the spiders. "*Don't* you *know* how *important* they are?" he cries emphatically, when I come in with an unread and rolled-up *New Yorker* from three weeks ago. (They stopped coming, a subtle sign that Sam had switched his mailing address.)

Noah is particularly attached to this one spider living outside our front door, in the upper right-hand corner of the frame. At bedtime, I tell them the one about Athena and Arachne. "Not a spider, but a woman! A woman punished for her weaving, a woman able to spin something beautiful from nothing!" But my daughter doesn't care. There is a warning here, about a woman so good at her craft that she is condemned to it.

It's odd, how having kids sends you back through the doors of your own childhood. The episode reminds me of running errands with my own mother, walking down a street that was home to many stray cats when we first moved there. They were mangy and daring—they'd dart out in front of you on the sidewalk, they'd peer at you from under parked cars. And there were hordes of them. I must've been close to the same age Lily is now. This all frightened me terribly, but my mom would make a habit of pointing to each as we passed and giving it a name: Fatty, Patches, and Colonel Mustard, to name a few.

For a child, this had a magical, calming effect. If my mother knew them, surely they couldn't be so bad. As an adult, I wonder if her habit was born out of her own fear, too. I think it was her way of making the new neighborhood feel like ours, of filling it with friends.

The next time we leave the house, I try a different trick.

"What if we name it?" I ask her. "And then it's sort of like an outside pet. You can pick."

She eyes the spider suspiciously. "Nancy," she decides. We welcome Nancy into the family, and then we quietly forget about her.

*

In the waiting room, you get to know people by their waiting room hobbies. Waiting room hobbies, I find, are never quite the same as your hobbies out there, in the world.

Your waiting room hobby, in a way, becomes your identifier, so you might want to choose it carefully if you think you might be there for a while. Something about waiting room hobbies feels terribly idealistic.

In most waiting rooms, there is, for example, always one (1) knitter. It's never clear what she's making; you can never quite catch the shape of the thing. In the corner, there's sometimes a woman snacking surreptitiously. The snacking woman is funny because she never takes her croissant out of its bag, choosing to "conceal" it in its beige coffee shop wrapping, as though she's not quite sure if she's allowed to eat in the waiting room. Instead of asking, she'll take nervous bites, bringing the pastry halfway up to her mouth and craning her neck like a vulture to meet it. There are also typically a few magazine grazers—very different from the one or two self-serious book readers. They bring their own. Though there is, at least in my doctor's office, one woman who has been reading the same plastic-wrapped library-owned hardback for weeks. Every time I see her, it doesn't seem like she's made a dent. I can't decide if she's a poser or a really slow reader, if she's merely distracted, or if she just needs something to hold. Perhaps she's grown really attached to the characters. Maybe she just wants to sit on the same page with them a little while longer.

*

When my youngest was still marsupial, I, like many parents before me, would hold the little rubber spoon and mimic a plane. I would fly the mashed peas into her mouth. Open up. What we teach kids is that their body is a destination.

When my youngest was a little older, she fought me on the greens. She wanted chicken nuggets. I told her that she was going to become a chicken nugget if she wasn't careful. That night, I showed them *Charlie and the Chocolate Factory*, Violet bloating into a blueberry. You are what you eat, I told them.

It's funny, the way we talk about the body. The heart, the brain, the stomach—things that are either full or empty, things that exist to contain something else. What I mean to say is it's funny, the way the body is just a vessel.

*

I stop seeing the woman who advised me about the letters, Linda. I can't tell if this is a good or bad thing.

*

Sometimes, instead of pulling from her usual reservoir of princess dresses, my daughter will ask to borrow something of mine. It's flattering, honestly. I feel cool. There's something enchanting about watching my everyday attire elevated to the level of make-believe.

But it's also odd, watching her swaddle herself in my cloth. The things she borrows are so baggy that they droop around her small frame. She drowns in them. I can almost imagine her growing in real time to fill the space. Sometimes I wonder if she's somehow acting out all the other names she's had. Maybe she's trying them on, trying them out—seeing who else she could have been.

*

When it boils down to it, an affair is a kind of dress-up. Trying on another life like a different cut of suit at Banana Republic, just to see if it fits.

In this alternate timeline, if Sam had met her instead of me, Maggie's friends would've *adored* him. They would tell her she got "the last good one," while they all rode around on boats and drank champagne on the weekends. He would've proposed on the water at sunset. They would've gotten married at a beautiful vineyard. There might have even been horses. The food would be gorgeous, if kind of bland.

Maggie's family would've *loved* him. They would have very wholesome American holiday traditions. Her mother would've knit him a stocking with his name on it and told him she knew he was the one for her daughter.

It all would've been so easy, so picturesque. (I guess, in a way, it's not too late for everything to fall into place for them exactly like that.)

The thing is, I've been so busy thinking about who Sam would've been without me. But if I could turn back time—if I could dye the grays of our choices, if we had never made eye contact in that bar—who could I have been?

A childless children's book writer; a mitigation investigator; someone who was closer to her in-laws, whoever they might be; a woman at the ramen restaurant/breakfast spot, sitting across from Darlene, same as always; surely still a cancer patient (some luck you can't change); a career woman; a woman worthy of being head-hunted; a woman at a bus stop; *the* other woman, maybe.

I don't really like to play this game, though, on account of Noah and Lily. I don't like imagining a fantasy version of my life that doesn't include them.

*

The kids are in the next room playing Trouble. The game's conceit is pretty simple. You are one of four colors: green, yellow, red, or blue. You're trying to move all your little plastic pieces around the board and back home as quickly as possible. The number of steps you can take is determined by dice that live at the center of the board, encased in a plastic dome. (Surely designed by a parent who was tired of losing dice.) When you click down on the dome, it rattles the dice for you, and pops up with another number.

One moment, I can hear the *click click click* of the dice and the subsequent *tap tap tap* of the pieces being moved, plastic on plastic. I'm in the kitchen trying to determine what might be conjured up with the things we have rotting in the drawers of the fridge. The next thing I know, there is crying.

Lily is at my side, screaming, "He's a cheater!"

Noah comes in with an "Am not!"

It goes back and forth like this for a little while. I hand them both Popsicles to stop the yelling, and after a beat, I ask Lily to explain, calmly, what has happened.

"Noah cheated to win," she says, licking the melty orange off her fingers. "He said he could double the number on the dice because he's older."

"I didn't cheat," Noah says, already done with his treat. He reads the joke on the stick to himself, laughs a little, then throws it away. I stop myself from asking what it said.

"That's cheating!" Lily says, indignant. She's started biting at her Popsicle, and it's coming off the wooden stick in little chunks.

The accusation is like a little barb through the heart. "It sounds a little like cheating, Noah," I say, surprised at him. A little mad at him, too. Apple, tree.

"It's not cheating. I just changed the rules," he says.

*

My son told me once that when trees get uprooted (by storms, by people), they feel stress. Even if you replant them perfectly, there is a chance the tree might not survive, on account of the transplant shock. It needs time to establish new root systems.

*

Maybe part of it is that I never quite snapped into place with Sam's family. In photos, I always stuck out like a sore thumb. As if I had been Photoshopped into the frame. Like the picture wasn't quite complete, not yet settled, the layers not blended.

Perhaps—after the loss of my own parents, walking myself down the aisle—I had hoped that marrying Sam would make *his* parents feel less like they were losing a son and more like they were gaining a daughter, when in reality they felt neither.

Or maybe he could feel how much I resented his family for the ease with which they glided through the world. We'd have a perfectly vapid time, and I'd complain about it the whole way home. Isn't that what you're supposed to do with in-laws? Mine were politely conservative with a silence on political matters and enough hours clocked on the East Coast to make you assume otherwise. They didn't smile with their teeth; all that money on orthodontic work—a waste! They never ribbed or roasted each other (the universal love language in my family, especially between my mother and me), and so I never knew where I stood with them.

The kids, however, *love* Sam's parents. Their affection was bought with hand-operated drones and dollhouses that towered over Lily. They were showered with gifts, hopped up on sugar, and allowed to roam free on the open acreage of the Moores' many homes.

They brought out the best of Sam's parents. Mr. and Mrs. Moore felt less like robots and more like human beings in the presence of Noah and Lily—their only grandkids. For this, I treasured my children all the more. Only Noah could get Sam's coiffed mother crawling on the ground looking for insects. Only Lily could convince Sam's stoic father to let his nails get painted by her wild and enthusiastic and outside-the-lines hand.

Ever since Noah was born, we visited the Moores out on Oyster Bay in the summer. Fireworks over the water for the Fourth of July. Noah, scuttling up and down the beaches on the hunt for seashells, which he would present like currency in exchange for another ice cream cone.

When Sam's mother calls to hash out the travel details for this year, I can tell by the tone of her voice that she already knows. She is gentler with me than she's ever been—a subtle shift that, inexplicably, makes me want to cry.

There are so many barely tolerable emotions one is expected to endure from a mother-in-law: condescension, hostility, resentment, envy, even straightforward hatred. But pity was not something I had ever expected. Pity puddles into that low register that people take on when they want to convey an unspoken understanding of your situation. There's that dip in tone, and the pity soups in.

In typical Mrs. Moore fashion, we only talk around the thing. (There is no elephant in the room! Look at how spacious and empty this room is!!)

But when we hang up, I sink down on the kitchen floor. Her pity does something to me. The final blow to the hinges barricading my sorrow. *The last time I would set foot in that summer house. The last time I would dry my face with a sun-warmed beach towel and steal a spritz of that sweet, earthy perfume that smelled sort of like tomatoes, which Mrs. Moore kept in her upstairs bathroom. The last time I would wake to waves or see the daylight slip away from the guest room.* Are you ever nostalgic for the way the light touches a place? The way the sun holds on to a room? Could you mourn the loss of that arresting sight—the way the light fingerpaints the wall with colors of its own, playful and daring and unselfconscious? The sunset throwing colors like a child before lights-out. One final burst of what's inside. *The last time I would see Noah's hair thick with sea salt, a little wavy like his father's. The last time we four as a family would collect cool-looking rocks or hunt for sea glass.* Now they'd just hand me pebbles as a token souvenir from their stay, and that day on the beach would be *the last time that rock looked like magic*; without the wink of the sun and the sea around it, it would just look like a hunk of earth in my home. *The last time I would stand on the shoreline and jump the tide with Lily or truly enjoy simply standing there as the water pulled away, shifting the sand beneath my bare feet*—it felt too much like the rug coming out from under me now, the ledge I was left on.

Mrs. Moore, for as long as I'd known her, kept her feelings about me perfectly level. When Sam and I announced our engagement, she merely patted me on the hand. At our wedding, she did not hug me. When I bore her first grandson, at the hospital, when she came to visit, she handed me a lovely bouquet of daisies and looked at me no differently than she had on the day we first met. She always treated me with abject indifference; it was a fact of my life, and it was this subtle change in the tides of her attitude toward me that truly threw me off-balance. Her change in feeling meant something really had fundamentally shifted and changed forever. Her pity, after all these years of the absence of particular emotion, marked me suddenly as someone outside of her family. Losing another set of parents. I had been cast in a new role, cast out. That new space between us was what the pity filled.

But there's something else to it, too. Mrs. Moore is the first person outside of our situation to know and reflect everything back at me. She is the harbinger of all the gentle hand touches and long, meaningful eye contact and lowered sympathetic voices to come. She is the first inkling of the story set free into the world, out of my telling, tumbling out of my control.

*

Before the melatonin kicks in, I lie in bed. There are no sheep for counting, no stories left to tell. Instead, there are two columns.

I divide my life into these columns. It's enough to drive a person crazy. It's like working dinner platters into the dishwasher. It's like a timeline, only I don't care about the exact chronology. I only care about the Before and After. On the left, we have the things from my life that I love, that are mine. On the right, we have memories I now feel I've been cut out of. Having your husband love another woman is like having someone in your house, only you don't know it. It's not a break-in, exactly. It's not violent like that, or all at once. It's a slow and quiet pilfering. Your flat-screen TV might still be there, but the small gold hoops you only pull out for special occasions— well, they're gone.

What is a bed if not two columns? I sleep on the right side, even now.

*

A commonly asked question about radiation therapy: Is it safe to sleep next to someone after a radiation session? (Yes.)

*

In the waiting room, there are sometimes "guest stars," which is to say not-regulars, lucky people with less of a tether to this place. Friends to help carry the agony, like Darlene. Family—devoted daughters who will eventually have to return to work and stop showing up. The sad truth of it is, for the patients who show up with friends and family in tow—no matter how loving or affectionate—there will always come a day in which they pass through the doors alone.

It's a reminder that even *this* could feel sort of routine, rudimentary. Inconvenient.

When it was my mother, I tried to think of it like a gift of time. It coaxed us into seeing each other regularly at a phase of our lives when that was no longer the norm for us. "Go to work," she'd chide when I showed up to accompany her to her doctors' appointments. "You have stuff to do." And I'd assure her that it was all taken care of. "You should be out with your friends. Don't you have friends your own age?" she'd say, shaking her head and laughing. "What's the matter? You don't like my company?" I'd shoot back, fake-offended. We did this little dance at pretty much every appointment: a ritual, a test almost.

In small ways, slowly over time, I watched her give in to the idea of accepting help. A small victory: a text from her that read, *Bring me one of those oatmeal cookies from that coffee shop near you*, sent the morning of an appointment. "Cancer loves sugar, you know," I said, handing it over when I saw her outside the doctor's office. "So do I! Something we have in common," she joked, taking a bite.

All those cumulative hours in the waiting room (and in transit to and from doctors' offices) reminded me of waiting in those hair salons as a kid, waiting for my mother to be restored to some livelier version of herself.

*

Packing the kids' lunches is one of my favorite parts of the day. I sit up at the kitchen counter and my own feet dangle, letting me be a detached kid for a second. Today, I'm packing their lunch for the last time in a little while. We've agreed to send them to Oyster Bay with their grandparents until things calm down. Mr. and Mrs.

Moore are *thrilled*. Mrs. Moore keeps calling me to tell me this. "We're just so *thrilled* the kids will be coming for longer this time! We hardly ever get to see them! Oh, we're just so *thrilled*." I'm starting not to believe her.

At the supermarket, I get a bunch of cookie cutters out of a sale bin. They come in all sorts of shapes. Any idiot can cut the crusts off a sandwich. I think it's much more fun to make the peanut butter and jelly be shaped like something entirely new: hearts and stars and Christmas trees and giraffes and cars. I make stacks and stacks of them, load up the ziplock bags. I know they're not going to eat all of them, but I can't help it. I nibble at the cut-away pieces.

*

Noah and Lily dutifully call me every night before bed for the four weeks when they're in Oyster Bay with their grandparents. They don't ask for any stories. They're the ones with the stories now. Stories about locals and neighbors and that one celebrity who owns a house not too far away from where they're staying, a house their grandmother (a gossip, another kind of storyteller) points out every time they drive past it.

*

There are things about Sam that I find myself moving from one list to the other. Traits or habits that come colored in another hue for me now. He is all about big swings, sweeping moments, Grand Gestures. After only a few dates, he'd send bouquets of roses to my office. Once he picked me up for our anniversary in a stretch limo that brought us to Olive Garden (the restaurant was my request). Giant, wooing moves.

He says I should keep the house. One last Grand Gesture. He continues to pack his things slowly, over the course of a few weeks. I'll go to the grocery or out to see Darlene, pick our kids up from their friends' houses and dodge questions from their parents about the waning state of my marriage, and when I return, a little more of him disappears each time.

He insists I keep the big-ticket items if I want them: the couch, the coffee table, the kitchen island. We bought them all fresh, shortly after he got the job that took him away from me. Our splitting is so painfully civil. And in the end, there are no giant gaping holes, only missing baby teeth the wind whistles through. A tchotchke here, a toothbrush there. He reorganizes the medicine cabinet and pushes all my potions farther back. At one point, you had to pull the mirror back slowly if you wanted something from the shelves; its contents were brimming, overflowing with life, and now it looks like parts of the house are receding from my touch.

We never did combine our bookshelves, so at least that's all intact.

Our kids are with his parents still. Of course we talked and talked it all through with them, so they knew more or less what to expect in a logistical sense, but we thought it might be somewhat traumatic for them to actually bear witness to our house picked apart and divided like this. The open boxes, an open wound. The beast of our marriage gutted.

For the kids, we agreed to experiment with an alternating week-ends schedule. We agreed that it made the most sense for them to stay with me for the weekdays. Sam would otherwise need to get a babysitter/nanny or (worse) his mother involved, and that didn't feel right. This was between us.

At first, he suggested taking them every weekend, but I protested. I didn't just want to be the homework checker and the lunch-box packer! I didn't want the bulk of my time with them to be relegated to the tyranny of school days. I wanted whole days with them! I wanted waking up early with Cap'n Crunch and *Scooby-Doo.* I wanted to see how the sun sat on top of their hair, their faces, at all hours of the day. I wanted to take them to the zoo!

From the hooks in our bathroom, we pull our whimsical, hooded terry-cloth towels, spoils from a drunken voyage to Target in our youth—me the shark and he the lion—and they too say their goodbyes. These wild things we used to be.

"I'll see you," he calls, from the mouth of the open car door.

"Inevitably," I say. "Friday, for the handoff." I'm not sure yet whether to be grateful or resentful that our kids bind us to one another in this way.

Sam nods and drives off.

When all that's done, I'm ultimately surprised by how little of his there was. Honestly, the place looks more or less the same. I just have more closet space.

After he leaves, I crawl inside our bedroom closet and shut the door. It's like my own little clubhouse. I make a ball of myself and don't move for hours. I blow my nose into my little shark towel. I watch the sunlight slip from the crack under the door with no way of stopping it.

*

Darlene checks in every night like a good friend. She calls when she and her dog are out for their evening strolls. Tonight, I'm complaining about the custody arrangement.

"So, weekdays with you, and every *other* weekend with Sam?" she clarifies. I can hear her muffle the speaker and gently chide Roberta for eating trash off the street.

"Yes!" I say, indignant.

"You're mad because you got the arrangement you wanted?" she asks. On the other end, I hear Darlene open her front door and pad up the stairs.

"I'm mad because he should have fought me on it."

Honestly, I'm surprised at how quickly Sam agreed to it. Sure, it made the most sense, logistically, but here I am barely okay with missing out on them every other weekend, and I'm mad at him for being so okay with losing them to the extent that he has.

*

The kinds of stories you choose to tell say a lot about you.

One night, as we were discussing their inevitable return from Oyster Bay, I ask Noah what he's going to miss about his trip. He tells me that his grandparents only tell them "nice" stories before bed. Swaddled stories. The kind with happily-ever-afters that end in a neat little bow like a noose around the imagination.

*

I decide to start growing tomatoes in the backyard, because it feels like less responsibility than a houseplant. The soil digs under my nails when I bury the seedlings from the farmers' market in the body of the earth. If I forget to water them, there's a good chance it will rain. It's like splitting custody with Mother Nature.

Mother Nature, as it turns out, is less good at protecting her young than you might think. We have garden pests of every kind. In my spare time, I wage war. I research deterrents, chemical and natural. I consider paying top dollar for an expert to come and deal with it. I consider getting padded mallets, gifting them to the children, telling them we're starting a real-life game of Whac-A-Mole. I put up a small fence, but it does nothing. Once, I pluck a tomato off the vine and leave it in front of the fence like an offering. Like, *Here. This one's for you! Please leave me the rest!* (He doesn't.)

Darlene says I should redecorate, something to mark the change. "Otherwise the days will just bleed together—old life, new life, what's the difference? This can be *exciting!*"

We spend the first half of the day rearranging the furniture. Then we spend the second half of the day putting it back. Turns out: we had a pretty practical arrangement, Sam and I. I tell Darlene that I *am* doing things. I take her to the garden. I show her the tomatoes with the little teeth marks. "See?" I say, pointing.

"You're . . . inviting rodents to come snack? Starting the first neighborhood initiative to end food insecurity for raccoons?"

I tell her I'm growing tomatoes so we can make pizza eventually, or Bloody Marys. We go inside and make them from the mix instead.

*

Getting to know my Maggie is a lot like getting to know a shelter dog. You kick off with all these warning labels: abnormal, aggressive. You tiptoe around the beast. Keep it at arm's length while trying to domesticate it, shape it into something you could call your own.

Slowly but surely, Maggie gets folded up into the royal *we*. When my kids aren't with me, I fling open the double doors of the fridge, and ask, "What shall we have for dinner tonight, Maggie?" I imagine her a much more decisive person than I am, with more conviction than I have in the rest of my body.

In college, Darlene taught me this trick for how to get through horror movies. She said all you had to do was narrate the scary parts. Just describe what you see. Maybe say it out loud, in a silly, singsong voice. *That masked man has an unusually large knife, and I don't think he was invited to this party!!* Or *Jack Nicholson definitely should've brought a jacket if he was going to run around outside like that! He looks cold!*

What I've learned from this is that if you say it in your words, it's less scary somehow. You cast your own spell on it. If I don't talk to Maggie, she's just this thing in my body that wants to kill me. The call that's coming from inside the house. But if I can call her Maggie, she's my accomplice. Together, we can decide what nature documentaries to watch, which red wine to open, if the dishwasher is full enough to justify running it.

*

I can't keep the hearts together. The artichoke hearts, I mean. I've decided to take up cooking new, adventurous things—things that are too exciting for children, for a husband. Things with anchovies! But not that.

Without the kids, my normal groceries go bad so quickly now. A loaf of bread could barely keep us for the week, and now I find myself throwing away so many moldy slices. I'm trying to shake myself out of my old supermarket habits.

I'm starting with artichokes. I cleave them in half like the Alison Roman cookbook tells me to. (I also make a mental note to get orange-red nail polish. If the Food Network has taught me anything, it is that that is the shade to wear if you are going to be touching food.) Trouble is: the layers slide off one another. Does this resemble the experience of loving someone? And why a heart? Why not an artichoke brain? Why is the heart the middle, the core, the reason?

And then how do we talk about the heart? With chambers, like it's a house, a place you can exist inside. ("You'll be in my heart," Phil Collins sang.)

See also: "The heart wants what the heart wants," as though it is entirely separate from ourselves. Maybe if we could just pluck his fickle heart out, I could keep the rest of him. I could still wake up to his cloudy, kind eyes and his dazzling smile with that one discreetly crooked tooth that he hates and that I love. I could go out to dinner with that full head of hair and his impressive height and his good table manners; I bet he'd still be a good listener. I could ride shotgun with his body in the driver's seat for the rest of my life. He the Tin Man, and I Dorothy—just a girl who wants to go home but doesn't know how to get there anymore.

*

Sometimes, when I'm all by myself and the house feels like it doesn't fit me anymore, I picture Sam in *his* new life, and I wonder if he ever gets lonely in it. If Maggie's off somewhere else, spoken for tonight, and if he ever misses the weight of my body on the couch next to him. If he's sitting in his armchair and it's maybe getting dark—does he have the impulse to pick up the phone and call? And if he did, what would he say?

Maybe: "I'm sorry." Maybe: "I made a mistake." Or perhaps even: "Can I come over?" Sheepishly, like in our younger days.

And then, early one evening when the kids are at Sam's, I'm microwaving leftover pasta for one when the phone rings—and it's him. The first thing Sam says is, "He's fine."

I don't know what to make of this. "He's fine," I repeat.

"Yes, Noah—he's fine. But we're at the hospital."

These words are far worse than anything else I could have possibly imagined myself. The microwave beeps aggressively, but I'm not hungry anymore, and I hear myself asking, "What happened? Is he okay?"

"He's fine. I told you that. He fell out of a tree. In the park."

"He fell out of a tree?"

So much of receiving bad or shocking news is simply repeating what has already been said to you. Like that shadow game that kids play.

"Yes, but he's fine."

"He's fine, but you're at the hospital?"

"Yes, and we need you to come."

"He's asking for me?" There is nothing worse than not being there. "Which hospital?"

"I need you to fill out some forms. What's his social security number? And our insurance group number?"

"Which hospital?" I repeat, and I'm out the door.

The cab ride is only fifteen minutes, but that is plenty of time for me to go from panic and worry to absolute rage. In the past few months, I have been sad, hurt, disappointed, afraid, embarrassed even. But mad wasn't really something that fully hit until now.

When I get out of the car, Sam is waiting for me out front. "Where's Noah?" I say by way of greeting. "Why aren't you with him?"

"He's inside. I thought you'd get lost," he says, leading me in. "This way." He puts his hand absentmindedly on the small of my back, guiding me, a reflex, but for the first time ever, I feel the urge to run from his touch. I pick up my pace, read the signs on the walls quickly, keeping a step or two ahead of him.

Noah is being seen by the doctor, and I am to sit in the waiting room and fill out the little forms. I know his social security number by heart. I have our insurance cards. After I hand all this to the man at the front desk, I sit down next to Sam. Lily is allegedly with his mother, who has been hanging around their pied-à-terre a little more lately, just in case Sam needs her.

It's a very different experience from the doctor's office, me in the waiting room, wondering about the other side of the door. How could he let this happen? How could he not be watching? How could he expect to do any of this without me?

"What happened?" I ask again, and Sam recounts a story about his adventurous little boy who just climbed a little too quickly, scrambled up to a branch that didn't hold.

"Was *she* there?" In the white noise of the waiting room, I have to ask. The two of them on a park bench. Sam with one eye on Noah, then, well, behold—the wandering eye! Was he distracted? Did he put her first? Did he put her in a cab home when Noah fell? Did she accompany them to the sliding doors? If she dared to be there then, how dare she not be here now! As if any other room was more important to be in than this one. Reflexively, I feel for my Maggie.

"Of course she wasn't there," Sam says. "I can't believe you would even ask me that. She has nothing to do with this."

I can't tell if my husband is simply that naïve or just so willfully ignorant. I'm hit with the immensity of how much he doesn't know. Health insurance details and the damage he's done. The gravity of the situation—could he be so high up on his own cloud nine that he feels immune to the weight of his actions? Not the Tin Man but the Scarecrow—a man without a brain.

Then, suddenly, Noah comes out of the exam room, so we drop the whole thing. It sits with us like an elephant in the room. "Are you the mother?" the doctor asks me, and I'm offended by this question. Can he not see the resemblance? The perfect pout of the mouth; the eyes—almost like I had plucked them out of my own skull and given them to my son; the unusually small wrists, one of which, the doctor tells us now, has suffered a very minor sprain. We should ice it on and off. To alleviate any swelling, Noah can hold his hand above heart level. He needs to wear a compression wrap. "It should heal in two weeks, three tops," the nice doctor tells us reassuringly. "He was very brave." Noah glows in the praise.

"Two weeks! That's nothing. You'll be playing baseball in no time," Sam tells his son. And I know that he's trying to make Noah feel better, but really, I'm thinking about how little this will affect Sam. In our trial run of how custody could work, Sam will only have to wrap that wrist once or twice.

Now, it's technically still Sam's weekend, but Noah wants to go home. "*Home* home," he says, and we all know what he means.

Sam accompanies us back to the house. In the cab, we sit three across in the backseat, and it reminds me of the time just before Lily was born, when we were still starting our family. When we were at the beginning of things. Once at the house, he lingers on the threshold like a creature that needs permission to enter, and Noah, of course, grants it to him.

"Can't Dad stay?" he pleads. Sam and I have one moment of telepathy, and I say, "Okay. Just for a little while."

We three go inside. I can see Sam taking stock of the very few changes I have made. He picks up a cluster of browning bananas off the counter and makes a face at me like he knows I'm just going through the motions of grocery shopping. If he were to open the fridge right now, he would see shameful towers of takeout.

"Do you have any ice cream?" Sam asks with the playful tone of a young boy, which comes off as whiny to me now. Besides, he's already elbow-deep in my freezer, pulling out the carton of vanilla bean. Yes, Sam has a bad habit of asking as he's doing.

The chocolate syrup, the sprinkles, the bowls and spoons and scoopers—all of that has stayed reliably put. We're making banana splits for dinner, and Noah is thrilled. Mostly through our feast, I say quietly, "See—some splits are good," and it does not get a laugh. Spoon sounds against plastic bowls. Sam clears the table, by which I mean he leaves the empties in the sink for me to return to later. At the last minute, full of ice cream and a second wind, Noah changes his mind about spending the night, and they both leave me.

*

When do we morph into creatures that resemble our parents? My kids put sweating cups of white grape juice on the coffee table, and I chastise them for not using coasters. It feels like something my mother would say, and I shine at that for a second before the kids want to know "But why?" If this is the coffee table's sole purpose— it's in the name, after all—why isn't it prepared to absorb what it is given? Also, they want to be able to count the rings. My son says that's how you can tell how old a tree is. You count the rings. He wants to be able to track his growth this way.

Why not? In a small way, every parent becomes an archivist for their child. In every house Sam grew up in, there is a closet with a doorframe that has his height marked in pencil. I remember the first time he showed me this, sheepishly—how he laughed it off as silly, threatened to take an eraser to it. I was so enamored by this personal way to mark time. My parents didn't own the apartment I grew up in, so we avoided marring the walls as much as possible. We were lifelong renters. Home wasn't a place that could be paid for and possessed like that. Anyway, someone else—another family, maybe—lives there now.

Instead, my mother kept my hair. In Cantonese, "hair" shares a character with "wealth." For this reason, you're not supposed to cut your hair on or after Chinese New Year—it would be like cutting away your riches. But my mom took this superstition and applied it to everyday life. We grew my hair out long for luck, as long as we could, and when we did eventually have to cut it (when it got unbearably knotty or dirty, or stuck with gum), she would tie it back in a ponytail and chop it clean off. She kept each cut in a ziplock bag, somewhere in the back of her closet.

*

Packing up and putting away some of the kids' belongings reminds me of something my own mom did during her annual spring cleaning sessions. I was a little older than my son is now. We didn't have a lot of money then. My dad was doing a small construction job for a Chase Bank in Manhattan at the time, and they were doing this promotion where they had little brown bears wearing white shirts emblazoned with CHASE BANK and the logo. When the promotion ended, the office manager found they still had a lot of these bears left. "You've got kids, right?" he asked my dad.

He brought them all home (much to my mother's dismay), and for every occasion (birthday, Christmas, middle school graduation), there was a brown bear waiting for me. Of course, they all looked the same and they stopped being a surprise, but I delighted in them every time, customizing them with what small flourishes I could—the T-shirt turned backward on one, a red ribbon around the neck of another.

There were dozens of them. And every year, my mom told me I could only keep the ones whose names I could remember. The rest were donated to the Salvation Army. And I learned to remember every made-up detail.

*

The morning the kids are due back from Sam's, I get up uncharacteristically early. Aside from our brief, contained ice cream dinner after Noah's hospital trip, the kids haven't been home since before Oyster Bay. I go room by room. I wipe down the countertops and take out the recycling. I vacuum, marveling at the number of crumbs I'm able to produce on my own. I put stray wineglasses in the sink. I make sure the TV is left on an appropriate, kid-friendly channel.

Tomorrow, we'll go back-to-school shopping at Staples with Sam. They'll pick out new backpacks and paper folders—and they'll bicker over which color best suits which subject. For today, I'm making and remaking their beds and placing a new little stuffed animal at the head of each one. A little tradition: an animal to represent my hopes for them this school year. For Noah, an owl: a vessel of wisdom. For Lily, a peacock: the ability to stand out and shine in a room. Maybe this year is for the birds, but maybe they can turn it around.

I'm upstairs in their room when I hear the front door open. "Mom!!" they scream. "We're hoooome!" The sound of them livens up the house. It's only eleven o'clock in the morning, but it feels like all the lights are being turned on. Sam waves goodbye but doesn't come in. After he's gone, the kids can't wait to hand me rocks from the beach. This year, they painted them with their grandmother. Lily hands me one that says *LILY* in purple in her bold hand. Noah's has eyes, like a pet rock. He says, "To keep you company the next time we're gone."

*

The kids are fighting with each other. It's been happening a little more often lately, ever since they came back from Oyster Bay and school started and they were forced to stand in the room with our new life. The guidebooks that I ordered online (too ashamed to pick them up myself in the store) say that this is completely normal: a reaction to the rift in their lives. It makes sense that they would "act out." (I guess the implied complete phrase here is "act out of line" or "act out of expectation." Behavior as a box we step into, or act out of.)

Today, someone moved a toy a little to the left and that, somehow, ruined the whole world-building thing they had going in the living room. The illusion shattered. The grubby hand that just wants to be involved. They are not speaking to one another. They make a show of it. It is this night that is the perfect night to tell them about "The Ten Brothers."

According to this old Chinese folktale, there were once ten brothers.

Each brother is blessed with a gift: a superhuman ability. One brother can fly. Another has an incredible amount of strength. Another brother can hear danger from miles and miles away, while another still has the eyesight of an eagle. Another can stretch and stretch and grow and grow, seemingly forever—to the bottom of the ocean, even! He would never drown. Meanwhile, another brother is impenetrable to the wit of the blade. And another still is impervious to fire. There might be others, but the youngest brother, I remember, could cause a flood with his tears, so the brothers always tried to keep him happy.

One day, their father is sent to prison by the cruel emperor. ("Why?" my kids decry. "What did he do?!" I pat myself on the back, emotionally, for raising children who question the edict, children who do not fear the iron fist that rules, who ask to see it turned over, palms open.)

In order to save their father, the Ten Brothers must embark on a series of trials—each one using his special skill and working together to save their father's life.

Of course, my kids are less taken with the idea of teamwork; instead, they want to know which characters they most resemble. Kids like zeroing in on a character—giving the story a clear focal point. They look for role models to shape their behavior, to shape the words in their mouths and tell them what they taste like.

"I like the one who can touch the bottom of the ocean," Noah says, and it makes sense for someone who likes the solidity of the ground beneath him, someone who wants to grow to meet the occasion.

"I want to be the fire one," Lily says. Her class has done the first fire drill of the school year. The kids were all hopped up on fire safety. Her homework that night was to come up with a family strategy *in case of an emergency*. "You should always know where the exits are," she tells me.

*

A week later, Lily is still obsessed with fire safety. After coming back from her dad's, she wants to talk about her secondary exit plan.

Lily is at an age when she can't yet imagine having been somewhere that I haven't.

She begins all her sentences with "You know." *You know how the lock sometimes sticks so you have to jiggle the key out a few teeth back, and then there's that really skinny long hallway after you open the front door? And if you turn right, there are the bedrooms, all in a row.*

You know how if you turn left at the long hallway, you pass the bathroom (blue), and the hallway opens up into the living room and the kitchen? You know how it's all one? And you know how there's this giant brick wall on one side of the room? (Lily is so taken with this: a brick wall—an "outside wall"—on the inside!)

You know how there's a window in the kitchen by the breakfast table? That's the one with the fire escape.

She's never had one before. She tells me her dad is growing basil (the easiest herb!) out on the fire escape in a little terra-cotta pot. She tells me that he let her practice climbing out onto it. She tells me, with an excitement usually reserved for Santa Claus or Six Flags, the way it felt to climb out onto the metal ledge. The way it shook a little under her step like a good old roller coaster might. The way it felt to be attached to home—*it's right there*—but to be in a completely different place. Not inside or outside, but a third and secret place. You know the way it feels to have the sky open over you?

*

Something that Lily insists on shuttling back and forth is a small cardboard treasure chest, about two-thirds the size of her body. Inside this cardboard treasure chest are a handful of princess dresses and other costumes, hand-sewn by me in a meek attempt to mirror my mother's talents, folded messily but with care by her. My daughter is at the age when she plays dress-up with a serious quality. "It's serious work," she told me once. She's methodical. She's got rules.

First, she washes her hands before handling the treasure chest. She does so for two "Happy Birthday" song cycles. (It's the only time she obeys this suggested guideline.) Then she *pat-pat-pats* her hands bone dry on the towel hanging by the sink. (Normally, she bypasses this step, flapping her hands wildly about like a duck slicking liquid away from its body.)

In both homes (or so I'm told, later), she keeps the chest in an elevated place, the highest spot she can reach on her own. We got her the chest for her third birthday. Most of the things inside have been spun into existence with my own two hands. Unfortunately for my daughter, I'm not the best seamstress. The lines are crooked. The hems bunch. At least they fit her specific self perfectly. That's what I tell myself.

When she takes the treasure chest down from its holy perch, she doesn't fling the clothes aside in a flurried attempt to find the one she's looking for, as she does with her normal wardrobe. She greets them one by one as she plucks them up by the shoulders. She's so careful that it almost hurts to watch. I can see in her slow movements the fear that something terrible could happen. I can see in my daughter the understanding that a single careless action can leave a stain or an irreversible tear.

*

When I'm alone, in the crater of our life, I don't let the silence fall. I bat it away with small gestures, like it's the balloon in Keep the Balloon Up. I become a podcast person. I am now learning to whistle, because I don't like my singing voice (too high). I even read *The Big Book of Anti-Jokes* to myself, hoping for a laugh to loosen the lump in my throat. I call a lot of old friends, who all seem to be wondering what the point is, leaving room in the conversation for the real reason I've called, waiting for the punch line to be delivered.

Sometimes I find myself just staring at photos of the kids on my phone, like I need proof that they are mine, that they were here, happy with me; proof that I didn't dream them up.

I buzz around the house, looking for little projects to tend to. I briefly consider adopting a cat or buying plants. In college, I took one introductory acting class (for shits and giggles, for easy credit) and the professor said that in every scene in a house, we should consider whether it's the kind of place where the plants are alive or dead. I don't know when we unofficially decided to become a No-Plant Household.

Hand on my worry stone. Probably for the best. Caring for a plant suddenly seems like too much responsibility for someone who can't keep sickness at bay in her own body.

And, of course, I talk to Maggie—my Maggie—the way one might talk to her plants, or her partner. It starts with me saying,

"Damn it, Maggie," after every doctor's appointment and after every call to schedule another. "Damn it, Maggie," after the arrival of medical bills that I tear open and hide in the top drawer of my desk, grateful, for once, for Sam's inattention. "Damn it, Maggie" when Sam makes polite conversation during drop-offs, and I have to concoct a convenient and believable lie about what I've been up to lately. *Damn it, Maggie*, a whisper in the hallway when I've just tucked the kids in and am thinking, naturally, of my own big sleep.

She becomes my scapegoat. "Damn it, Maggie," in the cookie aisle at the grocery store, upon realizing that they don't have the Pepperidge Farm Sausalito chocolate chip cookies with macadamia nuts. Because I wouldn't have even been walking this way, if it hadn't been for my latest doctor visit, I reason. It's all always her fault.

One day, after observing me shotgun a rather drippy vanilla soft-serve cone (with rainbow sprinkles) in the park, Darlene gently suggests that I start cutting out sugar, because even though there is *no scientific evidence* to suggest that sugar causes cancer, cancer cells (like all cells) thrive on glucose. Something I told my own mother many times years ago but had conveniently forgotten when it came to myself. Damn it, Maggie!

On the rare occasion that I have something healthy for dinner, it's "Take that, Maggie," because *surely* this salad I'm eating will have a healing quality, the power I need to eviscerate her. (Even though it's mostly mozzarella cheese and basil. It still counts!)

*

Sometime after Sam told me but before the divorce is properly filed—before the feral cat is out of its proverbial bag—there is a queasy period of time in which I know something irreversible has happened to me, to us, but I'm not sure how much to let the world in on it. Like maybe it's a jinx to put the cold, awful feeling situated in your heart into your mouth—to conjure it into a word. How awful are words! Siphons, thieves. Empty things, really, until we inflate them with our hurt.

During this time, I learn I really like lying. Like shoplifting ChapStick from the checkout aisle bin at CVS or raising your hand in class when you blatantly have not done the reading. There's a small thrill in it. Getting one over. During this time, I go to PTA meetings or out to drinks with other (married) friends, and I relish the make-believe. I can't stop myself from saying "my husband." My husband this, my husband that. Mine, mine, mine. A spell, a talisman. I invoke the "we"—because it feels like armor against our inevitable future. It's my way of warding off evil.

It reminds me of something my mom told me when we were visiting a second cousin who had recently given birth, about how in Chinese culture, when a baby boy is born, you should refer to him as though he is a girl, to trick the malicious spirits who are hungry for boys. (No one wants a girl.) At its core, the request was the same: please don't take him away from me.

*

Lily has described her dad's new apartment to me in such vivid detail that I start to dream about it. It always starts on her fire escape. I'm tapping on the window. From my vantage point, I can't see her, but somehow I know she's inside, watching TV in the living room with her dad and brother. From the fire escape, I can't see my family. I can't even see what they're watching. Instead, I watch the walls of the room turn different colors, flickering at the whim of the screen.

The volume is turned up, I guess; I can't hear it, and they can't hear me. In the dream, I watch them for an untold amount of time. Some nights, it feels like hours, and others, seconds. I always know the dream is ending when the sky gets dark. I tap and tap on the window with my fingernails, and then—I turn into a bird. I have wings, but I don't go anywhere. I peck at the fiberglass until I wake up.

*

I'll do anything to impress my eight-year-old. I research trees. I'll be a fountain of fun facts now. I tell him there's a tree in Athens, Georgia, that legally owns itself. The owner was growing old, and the city had been after his property for some time. He loved the white oak tree, and he wasn't sure if he could leave it to anyone who wouldn't be persuaded to sell the land by a tidy sum.

"What do you mean?" my son asks, incredulous.

Capitalism, a sad story for another day. I finish this one. The guy left the tree to itself. There's a plaque and everything now.

"What does it mean?" my son asks. "Do I own myself? Do you?"

The question reminds me of walking down the aisle alone on my wedding day. No parents left to stride alongside me. I gave myself away. The last few months have felt like a long and drawn-out process of taking back the pieces of myself from various beasts. I ruffle up Noah's hair—it feels so much like his father's—and I tell him: "Absolutely. And don't you forget it."

*

In college, I took a Psych 101 class in which the professor said that very few people have *genuine* memories of their childhoods. This idea froze me in my tracks; a robber in the night. Here's how you know if a childhood memory is real or merely fabricated from so many retellings: Look around your memory. If everything feels big, then it is real.

*

After the surgery date and time have been scheduled, circled without much ceremony on the aggressively autumnal September pages of our calendars, Darlene asks me, on the train, "Do you think they'll let you keep Maggie? Like, in a jar or something?"

People glance over with looks of confusion and mild concern. I burst out laughing. It honestly makes me feel better that she asked, because I'd been wondering the same thing.

There is not as much information on the internet about this subject as you might think. Are other people not morbidly curious? The best thing I could find, unguarded by a paywall, was a website for a company whose whole thing seems to be helping you store your tumor in their state-of-the-art facility. For an undisclosed fee, of course. Their website explains that your tumor could help guard you and your doctors against ineffective treatments in the future. It could contain lifesaving information if you learned how to read it. The body's Rosetta Stone.

*

Another children's book idea: a company that charges you an exorbitant fee and stores your humor for you. Saves it for a rainy day, when it might be better appreciated.

*

Lily is at the age where she has locked herself into a world of made-up rules. When we're out walking, for example, we can't split the pole or streetlamp. Everyone has to stay on the same side. She must avoid every sidewalk crack. (This one, she assures me, is for my benefit.) She must leapfrog from painted white line to painted white line as we cross the street; the blacktop is lava. *However*, we also have to make it to the other island of sidewalk *before* the count-down hits five.

So much about the way kids think is based around the idea that you can divine the future just by thinking about it in precisely the right way: if you hope enough, if you behave, if you are good, if you don't step on any cracks.

I want her to stay in this weird bubble of belief for as long as possible, so we abide by the sidewalk rules. We hop on the white lines to get from concrete island to concrete island. It takes us forever to go anywhere.

There's something in her devotion to these rules that sticks with me: the way you can feel like you have any control over anything. If you wish right at 11:11, it just might come true. If you cross your fingers, you are hoping, but if you hold them behind your back, it somehow makes it okay that you are lying. If you pull a soda tab back and forth and say a letter of the alphabet on each move, you can tell the first letter of your future spouse's name.

Lily comes back from school one day and proudly presents one such soda tab. "*G!*" she announces. "I'm going to marry someone whose name begins with a *G*. Be on the lookout." She carries the little metal tab with her every day for a few days. She keeps it in her pocket, careful to migrate it from outfit to outfit, fingers always fidgeting with it. It is her worry stone and talisman for maybe a week, and then she forgets all about it—until one night, a while later, she's asking me about soulmates.

It's on this night that I tell her and Noah about how, a very long time ago, all humans actually had two faces, four legs, twenty toes apiece. The kids shrink back in horror at this description of our lineage. One day, I tell them, the Greek god Zeus decided to cleave every human in two—punishment for our pride, or maybe worry over our potential—so that we might spend our whole lives roaming the earth, looking for our other half.

"So, you and Dad won the game, then," Noah says. Eight years old, and already thinking of love as a competition.

"What if we can't find our soulmate?" Lily asks, eyes wide with fear. I tell her another story, one that I hope will calm her.

There's a Chinese myth about soulmates, too. The way it was told to me: When you were born, you were born with a red thread tied around your ankle. It connected you, always, to your soulmate.

My kids kick back the covers and look at their ankles and glance back at me with only skepticism. "That doesn't seem right," Noah says.

And that's when I tell them the story of a young boy who is walking home in his village one day, when he is stopped by an old man. The old man is actually a god of matchmaking, but the young boy doesn't know this. The god disguised as a man tells him about the red thread connecting him to his future wife. He points at a girl in the village and tells the boy that, in many years, she'll be his bride. The boy is uninterested in love, and he doesn't like feeling like the fists of fate have closed in on him. He throws a rock at the girl and runs away. But when he grows up, his parents arrange a marriage for him. And when he pulls back the veil of his beautiful bride, there's a huge scar across her left eye and eyebrow. She tells him that when she was a little girl, a boy threw a rock at her, and it marked her for life.

"But it's a good thing, see," I tell Lily, who does not look satisfied. "You'll find your person because you're tied to them. You just have to follow your thread."

She drinks this in. "Are you and Dad soulmates?" Lily asks.

And I'm brought back to that first night in that one bar we haven't been to since. It's getting late, way past their bedtime, but I tell them one last story, an abridged version of this memory: Many years ago, there was a little bit of time when I was very, very sad because of losing my mother, their grandmother. "Do you remember me telling you about her?" I ask them. They nod. They know a little bit about her—not a person to them so much as a character in my stories. And they know about death—because of a class turtle incident Noah came home crying about last year. "Well, she had just died. And I was very sad. And every day, after work, I would go to this *magical* place that made me feel a little better. They had potions for happiness," I tell them.

"I want to try!" they both burst forth.

"When you're a little older, I promise."

I continue, "One night, two nights, passed in the magical place." Out of habit, I reach my thumb toward a wedding band that isn't there anymore. "And on the third night," I start to tell them, but stop myself for a second. I've told this story so many times before. With this exact rhythm, with this exact lilt in my voice. To all my squealing friends in the weeks immediately after, who wanted to know how we met; to acquaintances turned dinner and bridge companions and to Sam's colleagues at holiday parties; on our wedding day. To anyone who ever asked for our story, I realized, I always told it the exact same way—had heard it coming out of my mouth so many times that it felt fated, cast in stone, its own myth, the myth of my marriage.

It went like this: On the third night, there was Sam. As if by magic. He stepped into my life like a knight in shining armor; he saved me from my sadness. It felt like a sign, like I was being sent family, like he rescued me from some kind of wreckage when I needed him most. For someone so obsessed with endings, I realized with shock, I had concocted a Big Beginning that didn't really suit me anymore. *The last time I will ever tell it like that.* I do a hard pivot for the kids.

"On the third night," I tell them, "your father appeared." Like magic, as if *I* had *summoned* him. "I wanted a family," I told them. "And so did he." I told them that sometimes when two people want the same thing, it feels like a mutual spell is cast. "I think your dad and I *are* soulmates," I hear myself saying, "because we both dreamt of the two of you."

"Then why did he go?" Lily asks.

"Will you and Dad get back together someday?" Noah wants to know.

I put my best brave face on, and I tell them what I honestly feel: that our quest—their dad's and mine—was complete, that we, each of us, have many soulmates. And that they come in so many forms: in husbands and wives, in best friends, in dogs ("Does this mean we can get one?" Lily interrupts). And we're tied to them all.

"That's a lot of string," Noah says before I shut the light off.

All the world a giant ball of tangled string. Lines getting crossed. People all knotted up with the wrong people.

*

There is so much division in the self as it is. Why do we have to throw soulmates into the mix?

My kids are each half silver spoon and half service industry. Half homemade hands and half paying full price. Half clawed their way out of a rural province in China and half houses in several states. They are half of the stories that I put into them for safekeeping— and half something else entirely. Half something I don't understand. They're halfway to someplace, some privilege, I can never reach.

It makes me wistful for the brief blip of time in which there was not even a breath of air between us, when we counted undeniably as a single seat on a Delta flight: an economical oneness. What I'm saying is: there was a time when my body had two heartbeats, and for the longest time after that, it was like there wasn't anybody home.

*

I dream that I'm tearing through my own house—a strikingly accurate, down-to-the-last-detail re-creation of my house in my mind. Look, there's that runaway cherry tomato I couldn't find but was sure I had dropped earlier tonight while making dinner! Right there, partially visible under the stove.

I know this in my dream because I'm on my hands and knees looking for Maggie, or maybe it's Sam, or some lingering proof of them both. I'm rifling through trash cans. I'm opening drawers and rattling clothes hangers. Even in my dream, the shoulders of the coats slip off and annoy me. I realign them and continue my search.

In my dream, the sun is setting.

In the bathroom, I'm careful with the shower curtain. Could this finally be the nightmare in which there is a kind of killer waiting for me there? No. There is only porcelain and a small nest of my hair in the drain, and that is somehow more disappointing.

I start checking in all these odd places, like in Nancy's web and behind the blue-top Tupperware with the leftover tofu stir-fry in the fridge. I mean, I know she's a small-statured woman, but *come on*.

Under the bed, there are a few stray socks and forgotten toys. I stand back up and turn around and—oh! There, right in the hallway, at the top of the stairs, is a door I've never seen before. And there, and there, too. All these doors, leading to all these rooms. Each room is empty, except for the light, by which I mean all the rooms are full of something good. My brain makes up the soft light just right. Impossibly, it comes shyly into all these rooms like it wants to hold you. It makes shapes on the floor you want to sit in and shapes on the wall you want to frame. The light! In all these rooms of my house I never knew I had.

*

Before the back-to-school PTA meeting begins, a woman is adamant about not letting the kids play violent video games. She's confronting another mother, a woman whose brusque asides I've come to rely on during these things for a bit of comic relief, because her precious son came home from playing video games at their house, and didn't she know that first-person shooter games put all sorts of ideas in their malleable heads?

Meanwhile, I'm standing off to the side of the circle, trying to figure out where to look so it's not totally obvious that I'm listening. I've come to appreciate the predictability of PTA meetings: the petty drama, the way everyone paws inexplicably at your wrist in greeting or agreement, the bad coffee (watery and available in tiny Styrofoam cups, and I'm not sure which part I'm more offended by—the weakness of the coffee or the stingy portion sizes), the way they always end at least twelve minutes later than they're supposed to, when someone with nowhere to go says, "I just want to be mindful of the time."

I sip my bad coffee and the pre-show goes on.

"What're we teaching the kids with these games, really?" she demands.

Despite not liking this woman, her question is like an earworm in my mind. For the next forty-eight hours, I find myself thinking about all the games I've played with my kids and trying to extrapolate their meanings.

Hide-and-seek: the pleasure in being sought. Also, the fear. The horror in being found. The way the game teaches you to be invisible. To fold yourself into something. My kids contorted to occupy the smallest possible space. (Once, we found my daughter inside the cold hollow of the fireplace, curled up on the metal rack like a sacrifice.)

Hot and cold: like hide-and-seek with pawns and hints. The ability to tell someone to go farther or come closer by degrees. The dangling of communication, a way to control the actions of others.

Duck, duck, goose: sitting in a circle, waiting for someone to tell you who you are.

Tag: you're it. Someone has to carry the curse. (It's the way the diagnosis feels.)

I Spy: the fun of defamiliarization! It's talking around. It's not naming the thing.

Red Rover: a game about celebrating the strength of someone who can break a bond.

*

In the toy aisles of Target, Darlene and I are looking for presents for my son, whose ninth birthday is coming up. My kids aren't with us, but we've got Roberta in tow, and Darlene is pushing her around in a little shopping cart. Darlene seems to think that as long as she keeps Roberta contained in a tote bag, no one will notice. (Most of the time, she's right. The people who stop us most often are kids, wanting to pet the dog.) The linoleum floors are flecked with primary colors. There's a man on the loudspeaker asking some kids (not mine!) to stop riding the bikes around the store.

My son has never been big into action figures, so we stroll past the shrink-wrapped armed men with abandon. We step into a wasteland of board games. What are we teaching the kids with these games, anyway?

Perfection: the need to patch every hole, to find the right fit for every shape.

Candy Land: Do you remember the first time you got a "go backward" card in Candy Land? Who knew that was even an option? The shock of non-linearity.

Operation: a game about not getting too close to the edges of someone's insides. Rewards a steady hand. In fact, so many of these games for young kids are about exit strategy.

"What's Sam getting him? Do you know?" Darlene asks, and then immediately looks like she wishes she hadn't. *This is the first time I have no idea what present will be signed "Love, Dad." This is the first time in nine years that Sam has had to pick Noah's gift out by himself.* Poor Sam. Poor Noah! "Do you think Maggie's helping him pick a gift out?" I ask. "'Love, Maggie and Dad' just doesn't sound the same as 'Love, Mom and Dad.'" Darlene is eyeing me with a look usually reserved for her dog after she's just thrown up. A little pity, and a little like she's waiting to see if there's a greater outpour. "We'll get something better," she promises.

*

The night before Noah's birthday, I sit down to write him a card. All the ones in the store had *T. rexes* and trucks: the things we have apparently decided are for boys. I make him one instead. I'm no artist, but I freehand a simple tree with Lily's colored pencils. I give it eyes and turn its hollow into a mouth that says, *Hope you have a tree-rific birthday!*

*

From Sam, Noah gets Jenga, a game about knowing the weak points. Taking away from a solid foundation, without being the one to make the whole thing topple over. My husband is, unsurprisingly, adept at this. We play it together, as a family, with smiling faces in the spirit of Noah's birthday. Sam wins every time.

From me, Noah gets a tree encyclopedia, so he can easily know the real names of all the trees. He casts it aside on his actual birthday, which guts me a little. But then after that, everywhere we go, he walks with *Trees* from the Smithsonian Handbook series tucked tightly under his arm for easy access. Pretty soon, he knows all the trees in the neighborhood. He points them out as we pass:

London plane tree, thornless honey locust, green ash. One neighbor has a red maple in their front yard, which he appraises every time we pass. There are a few Callery pears—the ones that sprout little white flowers that fall like spring snow. "Sometimes people call them Jekyll and Hyde trees," my son tells me. "Because they're pretty but stinky."

The leaves are already starting to turn with the season, which I can tell is disappointing to Noah. Someday soon, they'll all be bare. But I guess that's still a little while off. Today, on the walk to school, he tells me about the newly planted sapling a few blocks over. He says it's a silver linden. He tells me they can grow up to seventy feet tall. It's funny to me, the way we cap growth and use it as a defining characteristic. "What else?" I ask. He says they attract butterflies. "And what do you think its name is?" I say. It's 7:41 in the morning, and my son already looks exasperated with me. "I just told you," he says. He drops my hand—he's never done that before—to reference his book. It's like his obsession has given him a new kind of independence.

"See!" he says, jabbing his little pointer finger at the page. "You can tell by the leaves."

"But what's its actual, individual name?" I ask him, trying for a joke, I think.

He doesn't say anything, just makes his eyebrows meet in the middle of his face in a deep furrow that reminds me of his father. "Have I *stumped* you?" I ask him.

He doesn't get it. "Silver. Linden," he repeats, slower this time.

"I don't know," I say, being funny. "It looks more like a Noah to me." I wink at him. He plants his feet firmly on the ground in protest.

*

The word *humor* comes from the Latin *humere*, meaning "moisture." The whole concept comes from the bodily fluids (the cardinal humors) that were believed to dictate one's mood.

It all begins in the body.

*

When I was very little, I dreamed of a small, portable pet—a hamster or something that would sit in my pocket and come along on adventures and keep me company all the time. I'd never be alone.

I remember being pregnant, sitting on the couch and reading a book and not being able to focus. My husband was working late, gunning for a promotion in light of our forthcoming addition. We hadn't told many people then. The baby was still the size of a peach pit. I was home alone, reading a book, and then I wasn't anymore. That's when it sank in. I had the distinct understanding that I wouldn't be alone—not for one minute, not for one second, not for several more months.

*

When I can't sleep, I find myself thinking of the woman in the waiting room—Linda—and her advice about the letters. Every time I sit down to write to the kids, I find myself wanting to write to Maggie instead. To tell her about my life—to prove to her that it wasn't deserving of being tampered with in this way. To tell *someone* the quirks about Sam—hard-won knowledge. Things that might save her sometime.

The Guide to My Husband: A User's Manual

He hates when his socks don't match. Also: he loves whimsical socks, but not whimsical ties.

He keeps a cold house but loves to pile on the comforters.

If he ever has a hard time falling asleep, rub his wrist in a slow, small circular motion.

If you ever want to win a fight, pause at the last thing he says and then say, "That's so funny. Your dad was just saying something like that the other day."

If he's ever snippy with you, but you don't feel like it needs to be a big fight, he's probably just peckish. Keep sour gummy worms in the pantry.

He has a favorite fork. (It's the littlest one.)

He likes his steak medium-well. (But in restaurants, he'll always order it medium-rare because he thinks it more manly to confront the bloody thing.)

Whenever I think of another one, after the kids have gone to bed and I've already exhausted Darlene for the day talking about the matter, I say it out loud. Quietly, just to my Maggie. I don't know why, but it feels suddenly like I have an outpouring of these tips and tricks, these fun facts of Sam. Like, *Look how well I know him.* Every bit a point in my favor in a game that no one else is playing. Maybe every lover becomes an archivist of their beloved. All these lodged memories rush to the surface, and it feels important to put them somewhere. I give them to the stone in my chest; it feels dangerously close to the heart.

*

Noah has a wild-eyed urgency about him. Everything is an emergency. He knows about the earth. These days, kids learn words like *extinct* and *endangered* earlier than they used to. He wants to see everything before it's too late. My son, wanting to race death.

It almost feels like he knows about me, somehow. Every time he says "before it's too late" and "while we still can," I feel the lump in my chest and fear my own personal extinction.

*

Sometimes I wonder if the cancer took something of my ability to be angry with the whole affair. If it took the bite out of me, siphoned off my venom. I think if enough bad things pile up, they inevitably cross over into comedy. I am a collector of bad things with the hope that I can make them funny. Midas and the Comical Touch. A woman gets left for another woman—it's tragic! She gets cancer on top of it—what else is there to do but throw your arms up in surrender, throw your head back and laugh? The hits just keep on coming.

For a lot of women, it's horrible to say, it happens the other way around. This is what I've gleaned from many late nights scrolling through the Reddit threads. They get the diagnosis first. They get to the outer boundary of "in sickness and in health." They get given a life sentence, a set amount of time. They get to say to themselves: the cancer scared him off.

The love of his life is dying. Surely he can't burden her with his newfound fear. Best to bury it in the body of another woman.

I have often thought of the body as a kind of burial ground.

*

In my mind, I've been expanding on "The Guide to My Husband: A User's Manual." I feel like I could fill a book with everything I know. What do you do with all the little details of a person you've collected over the years? Each little nugget like a treasure, a candy slipped into the pocket of your memory and saved for later. The little specks of shine (foil I mistook for gold) that I could pull out of my hat about any old lover! "Oh, I used to date a guy who . . ." A fun party trick. The phrasing of it—the way it centers the self. When you say a thing like that, you do not conjure the ex. No, you call a past version of yourself into the room for a little while. (Joan Didion said we tell ourselves stories in order to live. I think we tell ourselves stories in order to live different lives.)

Oh, I used to date a guy who only masturbated while lying on his stomach. Oh, I used to date a guy who was allergic to food coloring.

It feels so special to know these intimate glints of someone's day. But what happens when you build your home on silly things like this? Each glint of that person a brick of the house, a roof shingle, a doorknob. What happens when the tarnish sets in? In the right light (which is to say, the wrong light), the window's sash bars have rust, and you can see that the flue of the fireplace has been sealed shut. And the mold! A telltale sign of neglect. The floorboards give out with your step; there is nothing to hold you.

A magpie making her nest, a mother sewing scraps, only to wake up one morning and see her home for what it is: discarded aspects of people's lives, trash tied together with string.

*

Here's another one for the "Guide": Sam is a Beginner. He loves to *begin* little projects and does so with a fervor that is to be feared and admired, but be warned! He seldom finishes them. A non-exhaustive smattering of unfinished projects to date: rearranging the pantry, planning a road trip to Alaska, making a birdhouse, a lemonade stand on one hot summer day . . .

On this point, it occurs to me just how different Sam and I are. Beginners and Enders. He loves to start. He loves taking something that's existed and making it his own. He loves never telling the same story twice. Me? I'm the face on the other side of that coin: I'm obsessed with endings. I may not be the one to execute or act first— sometimes I feel like my life is simply happening *to* me—but I will write these endings in my mind: I am always telling myself *this is the last time* as a way of reminding myself to savor something—as a reminder that everything can be taken away. As a way of taking control over something I have absolutely no control over—as though I myself had penned and therefore *chosen* the way the story ended. I want things to be tied up neatly. No extra string.

Sometimes I think about giving this "Guide to My Husband" to real Maggie, really seeing this thing through. I can't help it. It's my nature. In my weirder imaginings, I mail it to her big corporate office: c/o Maggie. It'd find her. Other options involve skywriting, carrier pigeons, fortune-cookie fortunes, or faxing them to her, one at a time, every day. (That last option feels the creepiest and most serial killer-y, so I don't dwell on it.)

Most realistically, I'd print out the pages, watch them one by one. They'd still be warm to the touch when I slid them into a yellow envelope and arrived at her doorstep. I'd ring the doorbell and press the package into her hands. I'd say something cool and a little snarky and very knowing, like I was some version of her from the future. (In a way, I am.) Something like, *You're going to need this*, or *Good luck*, and then I'd moonwalk away.

What's most notable is that in all these daydreams, I have the last word.

*

I am lying on the exam table. Last night, I had a nightmare that I was in the wrong room, and the exam room I had stripped down in was actually my daughter's standardized testing room. There was a dusty chalkboard and an obnoxiously loud clock. We were all mortified. She did not pass.

When I woke up in the morning, I thought, *This is the last time I'm going to wake up with Maggie.*

In the real exam room, they pull up the curtain so I can't strain myself sitting up, trying to see. They put up the curtain, like they're the ones who need privacy, even though it's my organs poking out. I feel like one of those magicians' assistants in the shiny dresses about to be cut in half with a saw. I wait for the teeth.

I feel nothing below the curtain. I can't feel what I can't see—maybe that's the idea. My head is divorced from my body, like my husband is going to be divorced from my body.

In preparation for this day, I compulsively watched a video on YouTube of a woman who also underwent lifesaving surgery. Her setup was like mine, with the curtain and all, but she played the violin the whole time. It soothed her. One point five million viewers, the woman with a passion and a conviction so strong as to withstand the pains of surgery. It made promises about the human condition.

The anesthesia is starting to kick in, and my mind goes to my children's bedtime stories.

*

I'm assigned bed rest for the next forty-eight hours, minimum. I told Sam that Darlene and I were having a girls' weekend in Vermont, trying to sound interesting. It's the one state I know he's never been to.

Darlene has recently gotten a Photoshop subscription, so she can add a shine to the mediocre photos we take of her beautiful ceramics with our outdated phones. After some wine, we Photoshop ourselves in front of the Green Mountain State welcome sign; at the Ben & Jerry's factory; next to some cows; next to Bernie Sanders. The kids will never know the difference. What's a body, anyway?

They don't reply, they "react." They "♥" and "!!" At first, I was horrified. You know, the total disintegration of language, blah blah. But, turns out, those features actually make a delightful and satisfying pop. Especially the ♥—that right there, decidedly the new sound of love.

How much easier would things be if we could respond to real life that way? For instance, when my husband told me about her. There didn't have to be a conversation that felt like getting stuck on a rotary. There didn't have to be a swelling in my throat that came out like an apology, though I didn't mean for it to. Just 👎. 👎👎👎👎👎!

When my kids call to say good night, they don't ask me for a story.

Darlene and I decide to marathon *Gilmore Girls*, our comfort show, and we recoil whenever Lorelai and Rory put their shoes up on the bed. "Maggie probably has a shoes-on house," Darlene realizes in disgust. "We're going to have to make sure your kids don't pick up that habit."

In my morbid curiosity, there are so many other things I wonder about Maggie: If she came to our house, did she take her shoes off? Did she refill my Brita pitcher after grabbing a glass of water? Borrow a hair tie or two? (Or did I lose those myself? I'm good at that, too.)

When Darlene falls asleep, I open her laptop and internet-stalk Maggie for the millionth time. I take it one step further. I download pictures of her, from Facebook and Instagram. I Photoshop her into my wedding photos. I discover I love Photoshop. You can just undo things. There's even a Band-Aid tool. You can flip an image 180 degrees and tint it any color you like. If you're really good, you can distort the angles, drop a shadow. You can isolate parts of an image, make them their own layer, like existing on a different plane. What to put down first? What can we move to the surface?

Cutting around her jawline, getting the angle just right. I understand the surgeons better now, the control of the scalpel. She doesn't look half-bad, standing there with my husband.

*

My oncologist tells me I can't lift anything heavy for at least four weeks after the surgery. She says, "Wait a month, minimum, to go back to the gym or your normal exercise routine." I nearly laugh in her face. My "normal exercise routine" usually consists of walking into rooms and forgetting why I'm there, only to walk back a few minutes later. My "normal exercise routine" is several walks to the freezer, when I keep convincing myself I just need "one more spoonful" of mango sorbet. "I think that'll be manageable," I tell the doctor.

The only issue, I realize later, at home, is that the average four-year-old weighs roughly forty pounds, which technically counts as something heavy. Lifting my daughter is now a strenuous activity. For a whole month, I can't pick her up, and I can't tell her why.

*

Darlene is working on crate-training her dog. Now that we're going out more, she sees the need for this kind of discipline. She's tired of coming home to the mess, says if she wanted that, she'd have gotten married a long time ago.

To be perfectly honest, I'm not quite sure how Darlene ended up with a corgi. What she wanted was a big dog. A collie, something that could herd. A working dog. Something that would be useful. Then she came home with Roberta. They seemed content. I didn't ask questions.

To get a crate, we go to Petco, where the sliding doors reveal freezer aisles of "real food" for dogs and pretty, fresh-faced women try to tell us about the benefits of the raw diet. There are rows of kittens up for adoption and sweet old ladies in vests asking for two-dollar donations. Then we go downstairs, where they keep the lesser animals.

It feels like descending into something. I tap on the glass of all the habitats we pass, and Darlene shoots me a dirty look.

"They'll have to get used to it," I say.

"What? Kids? Childish behavior?"

I stick my tongue out at her.

The fish swim in circles, and I know how they feel. The hamsters burrow deeper under their paper bedding in heaps, and I almost want to curl in there with them. You can nearly feel the warmth of their closeness. The chinchilla eyes me like he knows I'm up to something. The lizards are shockingly docile. Most of them don't even start when I rap my knuckles against the glass, and that's how I know they'll be just fine.

Darlene has gone to talk to one of the women pushing organic dog food, so I keep meandering through the aisles.

There's one rabbit in the whole place. She's hopping around within the confines of a wire playpen on the lower level. Her handler tells me her name. The rabbit's name is Greta Garbo. The handler, whose name I forget, tells me she's going to let me in on a secret. She tells me that pet stores and rescue organizations give pets the names that will make people feel some sort of connection to the creature. (The year *Lord of the Rings* came out, every gray rabbit in a shelter was named Gandalf.)

The man in front of us in line is trying to convince the cashier that his purchase of two pet mice is entirely unrelated to his simultaneous purchase of a milk snake.

When Darlene starts assembling the crate in her home, I realize she has not given up on some of her dreams. She has bought the corgi an enormous cage, one fit for a large German shepherd. The corgi looks like a hamster inside it. Darlene doesn't mind. She looks a little pleased, in fact.

They say dogs grow to fit the cage they're in. People too.

*

Home alone, and I find a book of Baby's Firsts. It is that particular blue, light with the optimism of a newborn heir. It was a gift from Sam's mom (who, of course, bestowed on us its pink counterpart when Lily came around).

I had dutifully recorded all their important Firsts: *First Word, First Step, First Snow, First Birthday, First Tooth Lost, First Day of School.* These are the significant things in life, the book tells us.

We place so much stock in the first, I think, because we love to embrace novelty. *First Love. First Time.*

We relish the idea of breaking boundaries. *The First President. The First Man to Walk on the Moon. The First Asian American to Win an Oscar.* We want to be the first, to pave the way, to be a part of a long line in history.

The celebration of a first implies the belief that there will come a second. And then the phrase hits me: *First Wife.* It's the saddest first.

I clutch the books of Baby's Firsts to my chest like a shield against my sadness, like they are the antidotes to the endings I'm always writing.

*

There's a test they make you take after cancer treatment to determine the likelihood that the cancer will come back.

"Cancer: the sequel," I say to Darlene.

"No one likes sequels," she says back.

Here's how it works: If you score fifteen or below, your risk is low. Your odds are good. If you're in the sixteen-to-twenty-point range, your risk is low-medium. (Something about these descriptions reminds me of steak: medium-rare, medium-well, and you're cooked either way.) With a score in this range, additional precautions may be necessary/considered. Additional radiation, even chemo, is an option, but the risks may outweigh the benefits. If you score twenty-one to twenty-five, your risk is solidly medium, *but* the benefits of chemo at this stage *might* outweigh the risks. If you score between twenty-six and one hundred, you are prone to the cancer returning. My score—much like the rest of my life—was a waffling twenty-one. Cuspy. Blackjack! Lucky, in some cases.

My oncologist offers me the treatment reserved for the twenty-one to twenty-five group. She says I could be part of a study. They would track me, to see the side effects of taking this treatment in a relatively low-risk case. She says I could be helping other women: future generations. Lily springs to mind.

You never want to be the first in a thing like this. Suddenly, I'm afraid of the vast unknown once more. Sure, plenty of people donate their bodies to science. Good people! Noble people! Dead people. That "helping humanity" part usually happens after they're gone, no lasagna left in the fridge, no new episodes on the DVR, no unchecked homework waiting for your sign-off.

*

My son tells me that tilling soil is done during transitional seasons. He recommends taking fistfuls of earth in your hands and turning them over and over again; it'll help prepare for new growth.

*

One of the *very* early signs of pregnancy—even before the feared and storied morning sickness—is a swelling or tenderness of the breasts. The nipples become more prominent. They feel heavier.

This change can occur as early as ten days after conception. Morning sickness occurs four to six weeks in. It begins with the breasts.

There's something kind of amazing about it—the instinct of the body. My breasts don't need to read dozens of WebMD articles or Reddit forums to know what to do. The body is simply equipped to take care. It is programmed for survival. First, its own survival—then that of this other thing.

As a generally small-chested woman, I have never really been all that aware of my breasts. ("You're lucky," my bosomy friends tell me, "that they don't flop to either side of you when you lie down on your back for sleep, for sex.")

But when I was pregnant with both of my children, it was the breasts that were the first telltale sign. *Tender* is the word a lot of people on internet forums have used to describe the sensation. I hate that word. Outside of breasts, we only ever use it to describe meats. Tenderize the meat. Chicken tenders. It is a violent act; it is a product. But, sure. When you're pregnant, your breasts become tender to the touch. Also, the veins. This is—according to one of the many incredibly vague articles on the subject that are supposed to help you distinguish between PMS and pregnancy—one of the key differences. While you may experience soreness in both cases, if the blue veins in your breasts become prominent, it is more likely that you are, as they say, with child.

When I was pregnant, I was made to be acutely aware of my breasts, my purpose as a milk provider. My breasts gained an agency.

They made themselves known! Once a more sentient part of my body, they couldn't slip quietly back into the background. They created a new life with a mind—a malice—of its own.

When I was pregnant, I couldn't believe what my body was capable of creating. When Noah and Lily were born, it was like they took the best parts of both Sam and me. When my body is left to its own devices, when it makes something up entirely of me, it makes a time bomb. It makes me feel like Sam is responsible for how good the kids turned out.

*

Darlene and I take slow, easy walks with her corgi in the afternoons of my healing while the kids are at school. Roberta is afraid of everything until you put a leash on her. Then she's a new dog, bounding down the sidewalk, barking at bigger dogs, running squirrels up trees. The thing Darlene and the trainer are working on now is how to get the pup not to pull, to stop her from darting wildly at every whim. You're supposed to stop in your tracks every time she tugs, until she walks back to you. We must look ridiculous, with all our starts and stops, the way they tell you to walk down the aisle at a wedding.

Darlene knows better than to tell me I'm lucky. Instead, she says I have a new leash on life.

*

The largest tree in the world is the General Sherman, if we're measuring by volume. It stands 275 feet tall, with a diameter of thirty-six feet at the base.

According to *Guinness World Records*, the tallest living tree is a sequoia in Redwood National Park. It was given the nickname Hyperion: a Titan out of Greek myth, the father of the sun god, Helios. (Inside this fun fact is the belief that only exceptional things are worthy of being named. I bet the tree right next to Hyperion lives and dies an anonymous life.)

The precise location of Hyperion is kept a secret in order to protect it. This both soothes and saddens me at once. Like, we just know people can't be trusted with the whole truth.

When Darlene asks me why I haven't told Sam about the cancer yet, I'm not sure how to answer. They say that near-death experiences change you. They make you more appreciative of what you have. Maybe weaker, maybe stronger. In the particular case of Sam, I am changed in the face of this experience in a different way. It has turned me into someone who can keep a secret from the person who knows all my secrets. It has turned me into someone who can separate her life from her family's and still survive.

*

Magpies are considered some of the world's most intelligent creatures because they pass the mirror test, a scientific study that prizes the ability to recognize yourself.

I have always been a little mirror-shy, ever since my mom told me about the demons lurking there, pretending to be my reflection. But when I think of my mom, I always picture her as she was in that hair salon, after getting her hair dyed, with the Mona Lisa smile of a woman who sees herself.

*

In most cultures, there seems to be a myth about people who weren't supposed to fall in love. It's seen as a noble thing—a love the world might bend its rules for, a love worth telling the story of.

The story I'm thinking of tonight has to do with magpies. The way they swarm to form a bridge between the earth and the heavens so that two lovers may meet for one night only.

This is the story of Zhinü—the goddess of weaving. She was the daughter of the Jade Emperor, rumored to have created his robes out of threads she pulled from the clouds. My daughter loves this detail, wants to wrap herself in weather, too.

At this point, Noah interrupts me. "Haven't we heard this one before?" I've told them all about the goddess of weaving already, they tell me. "The spider lady!" Lily says. We know her story.

I tell them there are many weaving women. Or maybe there really is only one, but everybody carries with them their own version of the same people.

This somehow satisfies them, and we go on:

The goddess has come down to earth and is bathing in the river when a humble cowherd lays eyes on her and, so captivated by her beauty, instantly falls in love with her. He steals her clothes—her only means of returning home to heaven. But Zhinü falls in love with this small-time thief. And, you know what, she marries him.

My kids protest this point, too. "Why would she fall in love with a man who stole from her?!" they shriek. I tell them it's because she isn't as smart as either of them, a compliment that delights them.

When the Jade Emperor finds out about their nuptials, he is outraged. He calls in a favor from the divine immortal Queen Mother of the West. He asks her to bring his daughter home, which she does.

To make their reunion even more impossible, the Queen Mother of the West creates the River of Heaven to further separate them. "We know it as the Milky Way," I tell my kids. They press their faces to the window, but the city lights hide the sight from us. Heartbroken, the lovers become stars.

It strikes me in these tellings how many of our tales are desperate attempts to put the stars in the sky. These stories are our grasping at straws that were drawn long before our time.

Eventually, the occasionally benevolent Queen Mother of the West lets the lovers meet for one night a year—and magpies swoop in to create a bridge over the River of Heaven. "It's like Chinese Valentine's Day. It's called the Qixi Festival—celebrated in August." Lily looks disappointed. "We just missed it," she says. "Next year, we'll remember," I promise. I kiss them good night. "Keep an eye out for magpies," I say, turning off the lights.

And in this story, I confuse myself. I'm not sure who I am in it.

I spend the rest of the evening trying to keep the symbols straight. Trying not to mix my metaphors. In Chinese culture, the humble magpie has come to represent the impossible relationship between men and women. Check. In science, magpies are the epitome of intelligence because they can recognize themselves. But also: they eat trash. They are known for their songs. In Europe, they have a bad reputation for being thieves; for finding shiny objects and taking them home.

*

When the kids aren't with me, I call those my "off weekends." When they roll around, they seem to stretch out before me like a desert of time. The sand can't squeeze through the hourglass quickly enough.

To stop myself from going totally insane in our house, I go to the coffee shop around the corner—the one where the baristas know us. I order one large cup, and I see the owner pick up two like a reflex. "Just one," I say quietly. She nods and says, "No Sam today?"

There's a family sitting on the couch by the door when I walk in. It always *looks* so cozy, but I know better. Why do we put soft fabrics in public places like this? They're so hard to clean. Even now, there's a young kid scrambling on the couch, dropping croissant crumbs everywhere and kicking his little sneakers against the armrests, where some student will surely nod off later, not knowing all that has occurred here. The mother looks up at me, somewhat apologetically, and I realize how I come across to her. Alone now. None of the markings of marriage or motherhood.

*

When is the right time to let other people in on your life? When you get engaged, it's pretty common to scream it from the rooftops as soon as possible. You're expected to tell everyone you've ever met immediately. If you don't, something must be wrong. Like in this silence—that's where the doubt lives.

When you first find out you're pregnant, it's the complete opposite, because of the concept of jinxing it. You really don't want to tempt fate by bragging about the miracle of life. (We are okay with tempting fate on the miracle of love, though!) You're supposed to keep it a secret for the first three months. Sam was very bad at this. In those days, I saw it as an expression of his excitement—a love and a fervor about our future that could not be contained. He wanted to let everyone in.

His family was ecstatic. His mom called with well wishes—and a litany of pregnancy reminders, to-dos, health tips. She wanted to come over and pack our go bag. Then she wanted to buy us new stuff for the go bag when she saw the ratty things I had. She wanted to tell me about Sam being born. (This part I loved.)

The rules for things like divorce are a little less clear. There are fewer guidelines on when to tell people.

There are, however, signs that the news has hit the PTA. I don't know if it's from the kids telling their friends of their new split home or maybe something mentioned by Sam in passing to another parent, but the moms look at me with softer eyes. The two single dads in the group seem to hang back after pickup in case I want to "talk."

When I was growing up, my parents were terribly private people. Anytime anything bad happened, they hid it from you, and if you happened to sniff it out, they made you promise never to tell anyone outside the family. When my mom got her diagnosis, she hid it even from her closest friends. "It's silly superstition," she said, when pressed. "In case the bad luck is contagious."

*

The divorce papers came via a lawyer. (Don't you love encountering lawyers? It makes you want to use words like *via* for the rest of the day.) It was, I'll admit, a real slap in the face, considering I had seen the coward not two hours prior to pick up the kids.

What's with lawyers saying, "You've been served," anyway? My (ex-)husband picks up on what feels like the thousandth ring. He takes so long to pick up the phone that my mind has drifted. I miss the tether of an old-school phone cord, the kind that loosely resembles the spines of spiral notebooks. I want my fingers to have something to loop around. It's ringing. I'm wringing my hands. When he does answer, what I say is the thing that was already on my mind.

"What's with lawyers saying you've been served, anyway?"

His breathing is quiet, shallow. "You got the papers." It isn't a question, so there isn't anything to say to that, really. So I go right back to my original point.

"I mean, 'served' implies a kind of service—preferably one requested by the party in question. You sit down at a diner and you get served. Coffee and cherry pie. That's the kind of served I want to be."

He's not sure what to say to this. Best to just wait it out. At least he's learned something during our marriage.

I go on. "Unless it's like that *Twilight Zone* episode where it's *you* who's on the menu! I've been served. Well, that feels right, actually." Then I hang up. All sorted.

I call Darlene next, naturally. There's a knock at my door in less than half an hour. Roberta trots in behind her and plops down beside us when we sit. There's nothing on the dining table except for the papers. They're flipped open to the last page. There's even a little pink neon sticky where I have to sign, like the lawyer thought I might be some kind of idiot. (Maybe I am.)

There it is. The blank line. So final. No Sam today.

"Do you remember being twelve and dedicating an inordinate amount of time to your signature?" I ask my friend. Trying to figure out if you should cross your *y*'s or if you should have a heart over the *i*. You imagined signing autographs. You never thought you'd be using that signature for something like this. The whole scene reminds me of Lily's favorite movie, *The Little Mermaid*. And what's a signature, anyway? Proof of the power of a name. All you have to do for something to be legally binding is sign. A name is a promise.

Darlene takes a pen out of her purse and slides it across the table in silence. Roberta politely gnaws on a chair leg.

"I remember your first date," Darlene says, after a little while. "Courtship-side seats," she muses, a callback to her wedding toast. It seems like not that long ago. Can so many of these things have already happened to me? A whole marriage, two perfect kids, a generous alimony agreement, and a very polite custody battle.

"And now you've got divorce courtside seats."

I pick up the pen. It's awfully *ordinary*. Nothing ceremonious to it. Just sign your name like you have a thousand times before, right next to Sam's. I run my fingers along his signature, the curves I know so well I could forge them in my sleep. The ink doesn't budge. The myth of the demigod: the blood on the page that sets everyone free.

After I sign the papers, Darlene wants me to practice saying the words "my ex-husband." She has me repeat them like I do our phone number and street address with the kids, just in case. My ex-husband. My ex-husband.

Once I've got "my ex-husband" down pat, she makes me say his name, plain and simple. "I've said his name thousands of times," I tell her. "What good is that going to do?" Darlene tells me that the point is to cut myself out of his identity completely. Eliminate the "my." Not my husband, not my ex-husband, not my anything, no not mine.

*

Sam calls. It's a Thursday, around two p.m., which means he must be calling on his (late) lunch break, the way he always used to. Why? He wants me to meet his Maggie.

"I think you're actually really going to like her," he says.

I hate it when people say this to me. Even outside of this specific situation, I have always hated people telling me this before introducing me to someone new. It gives me no reassurance. I'm sure I'm going to like whomever it is; who cares? The real question I have: Are they going to like *me*?

"I'm really going to *like her*?" I repeat back. "Try again."

"Don't you think it's time?" he says.

Sam has a terrible habit of doing this—taking his own opinions and dealing them out like a deck of cards, flipping them over in front of you and forcing them into your hand.

A negative space I had always been happy to fill.

I file this observation away for "The Guide to My Husband." What would it be like to actually put this manual together, to hold its weight in my hands and to hand it over to Maggie? A tangible measurement of our relationship. *This* is how much I know and how much I have learned and how much I have loved.

At this point, he and Maggie have been dating for roughly eight months: the same amount of time it takes to create a whole human life. The same amount of time it took me to fall helplessly in love with him. Where were we eight months in? In the optimistic shine of our twenties, practically living together by then, a stage of love in which you look at your person day after day and say, "I can't believe I found you," like it's supposed to be some sort of accomplishment; a stage in which you can't keep from pawing at one another, needing the assurance of touch to know that this shimmering being before you is real.

Over the phone, Sam says, "We're going to move in together

eventually." Less a distinct choice and more an unspoken inevitability, it seems. "Our kids will, at some point, be spending a considerable amount of time with her. C'mon. Just one drink?"

"Can it be at Six Flags?" He laughs; I relent.

*

My son has to make a family tree for school. It's one of those little get-to-know-you activities that teachers like planning at the start of the year. This excites him. He spends hours with the tree dictionary, trying to figure out which kind our family most resembles. After dinner, the kids both tucked in upstairs, I sit at the counter and look over their homework. It's a small nightly ritual I didn't know I would love about being a mother: seeing their thought process spilled across the page, noting their progress, and the small changes in the way they write their names.

Noah tells me that when it's his dad's turn to do the homework checking on Sunday nights, he flags their mistakes, which he prompts them to change over breakfast in the morning. Me? I leave them be. I uncork a fifteen-dollar bottle of white wine, and I pick the burnt-but-still-salvageable bits off the lasagna pan.

On a family tree, most children make themselves the trunk; they locate themselves as the central point. But not my son. He's put his parents there, instead: a bifurcated tree, split right down the center of the bark. It knocks something out of me.

It's in the roots that he remembers his grandparents. The underground system is quite extensive. It reaches far into the ground. It looks like a family tree turned upside down. There are my husband's parents: Mr. and Mrs. Moore. I hold the page closer to find the people I might recognize. On my side of the family, the names are in Chinese. It's hard for my children to understand. When he got home from school today, he had me write out the names of my parents and their parents as far back as I knew. I pinned the characters to the page the best I could. Squinting, I think I can make out some of them. His lines lack intention. They're just markings on the page, empty of meaning. (It's my fault. I never sent them to Chinese school.) In his sloppy, slanted little-boy handwriting, my side of the family is tangled there, in the roots.

He labels himself a mere leaf in the wind. And there is his sister. A sad tree in the dead of winter, with two leaves just barely hanging on.

He gets a B+.

*

"How are you feeling?" Darlene asks cautiously on one of our walks.

"Un-Moored," I say, joking and not.

*

I never rinse my mugs out anymore. What's the point? If you drink your coffee black, is it not just water atop more water? This lazy allowance, I think, should be my reward for not adding half-and-half. After a few days, the rings appear, like the shorelines that shift in the sand throughout the day. The insides of my mugs look like cut-open tree stumps. I make a mental note to tell my son. Maybe my insides look like the insides of an unwashed mug look like the sliced stump of a tree. Could they see my growth when they cut me open? Did it count?

*

"What if you end up really liking her?" Darlene cautions me over the phone. "Meet her, and we won't be able to vilify her in quite the same way anymore. She becomes a real person."

"She is a real person," I say. "A real person practically living with my h—Sam."

"Attagirl."

Although I adore Darlene for her vitriol and sorely need it most of the time, I also know it's unfeminist of us to hate Maggie. Actually, I don't. Hate her, that is. It's more like I'm fascinated by her. Obsessing over her is like falling in love with Sam all over again; I'm hooked, drawn closer. Because, really, Maggie and I share an experience that very few people on this earth—not even Darlene—are acquainted with the feeling of. Maggie, too, knows what it is to be under the warm, flickering heat lamp of Sam's daily affection, to be in her skin in this new way.

There's a part of me I've been trying to bury deep down under the soil of blanket resentment. The curious gopher wants to know: Did we fall in love with the same parts? Did she notice the same small things, like the way he always keeps both pen and mechanical pencil in his front pocket; the way his eyelashes are so long they get tangled up in each other sometimes in the messy beige morning? Like a puzzle in one of those *Highlights* magazines hanging around in children's dentists' offices all over the country: Who found the most treasures? Which did she spot first? The Rorschach test of love.

*

There's one bedtime trick Sam used to do that the kids found funny and felt betrayed by in equal measure. (They told me so.) He wheeled it out when he was too tired for stories.

"Once upon a time, the end."

*

A man and a woman and another woman walk into a bar. They all say, "Ow!"

The first time I met Maggie, it was at this German biergarten we used to go to all the time, before marriage and kids turned us into our homes.

I got there uncharacteristically early, which is to say right on time. (Okay, I probably would've been late had I not had to drop Noah and Lily off for a play date just a few blocks away.) At five p.m. sharp, the bar had just opened, which meant I had my choice of picnic tables. It was good to face the door, to be able to see your enemy coming. I moved twice, ultimately to the seat in the corner by the window. I took my hair out from the jaws of a comically large plastic clip. Then I put it back up and then I let it loose again. Everything about the way I wore myself felt wrong. I tried to catch a glimpse of myself in the reflecting glass, but it was still too bright out.

And then there they were.

How strange it was to see the other Maggie. (Darlene made me stop referring to her as the Real Maggie: "Was your Maggie not real, too? The doctors held Tumor Maggie in their hands! That Maggie almost cost you your life.") She was taller than her headshot and profile pictures let on. She stood nearly eye to eye with Sam, an even match.

I swear I felt a cold absence in my chest, where the tumor used to be, or maybe it was just my heart, turning away from the sight.

"Maggie, right?" I reached out a hand. I'd gotten so used to saying her name in the warmth of my home, but it hurt in my mouth then, like a cavity. The cavity in my chest, the cavity in my marriage. Rot making a home in the hollow.

At the bar's counter, Sam got an IPA, and I opted for a sour. Maggie got white wine. Sam quickly offered to pay for us all. "All on one," he said, handing the bartender his card. Old quick draw. But I insisted on getting my own. I took out my credit card, and I placed it solidly on the counter. It was a new one, from a bank Sam didn't have an account with. He seemed caught off guard, for once. I took a small satisfaction in that.

Then we all sat down, them across from me: two against one. (To be fair, there was no possible seating arrangement to make this meeting any less awkward.) Even with a few feet of wooden table between us, Maggie's hands smelled like oranges. Don't you just hate that? Name another fruit whose scent perfumes you like that. It's like bragging. You always know the healthy eaters because their hands always smell like oranges. Yes, a habitual orange-eater is the most annoying thing a person can be.

"You smell nice," I told her.

Our little group went on exchanging dumb, obligatory pleasantries for the first few minutes, about the unpredictability of the weather "this time of year" and our annual shock at the way the days get shorter. We collectively experienced the temperature! We were all indignant about the light being stolen from us! A way for us to be on the same side of a stupid story. We read the little table advertisement about Oktoberfest out loud, for lack of anything else to say. "I'm not a big beer drinker, really," Maggie said, gesturing to her wine, and I thought I saw a glimpse of disappointment in Sam's eyes.

The bar had these truly giant pretzels, and I ordered one "for the table," which really meant for me, but sure, everyone could have some.

It gave us something else to talk about: the goodness of the pretzel. "The pretzels are really good here," I said.

"They're huge," Sam chimed in.

"Massive!" Maggie, getting carried away, said. Her orange hands tucked into it. The pretzel opened the debate about whether we should consider the potato pancakes with applesauce on the side as well.

Sam is usually the focal point of every room he walks into. On that day, though, he receded into the background, took on the role of audience member instead of active participant. He kept looking at me, then at her, then at me again, as though this were a heated tennis match. I had never really seen Sam nervous like this. His left leg bounced up and down with anxiety under the picnic table, a quiet but very persistent and annoying old habit, and I had to stop myself from placing my hand over the top of his knee to calm him. A few moments after I had the instinct, I watched Maggie do this instead.

Honestly, I was half expecting our table to flip over from the weight of the elephant in the room.

When Sam got up for the bathroom, I thought, *This is it!* I thought she was going to lean over and say something full of sorrow. She would apologize for the way this all shook out. She would say something we both knew to be a lie, something like *I really hope we can be friends.* She pitched forward and said sweetly instead,

"You've got a bit of pretzel in your teeth." Pretzel in my teeth, egg on my face. Sure, what else is new? I think briefly of Wu Gang murdering his wife's lover.

"Thanks," I think I said, and because I'm a whole moron, I added, "And I love your shoes, by the way!" (They were fine.) The whole evening, I couldn't stop complimenting her, for lack of something to say. There was that need to fill the void again: recognizing an emptiness and seeing yourself fit inside it.

Having an awkward conversation with someone you don't know all that well is an awful lot like having a child first acquiring language. You don't know how to talk about what's not in the room, right in front of you. You are stuck in the lines of where you are, limited to tangible beasts. The physical world unfolds without its second skin, not yet overlaid with the complexities of feeling. It's all pointing and calling the sky the sky.

When my kids were first splashing in the stream of language, it was like Adam naming the animals: cat, dog, Mom, and Dad—the first time they correctly named us, it was like being brand-new, the slate wiped clean, the unexpected desire to only be a person as perfect and pure as the word bubbling from their little mouths.

(My favorite time, though, was when certain words were too unwieldy for them, when the kids couldn't pronounce certain things, and "spaghetti" became "noodle" became "noo-noo." A family makes up its own language that way.)

At the bar, Sam returned from the bathroom with (of course) a knock-off Jenga set called Jumbling Tower. He, too, clearly felt we needed a centralized activity. It was something to do with our hands, now that the pretzel was consumed. Together, we built the structure and picked it apart block by block.

Later, when I told this story to Darlene, she wanted to know who knocked it over in the end. Truthfully, no matter who it was, it seemed like a metaphor I didn't necessarily mean, so instead I just said that we had a fine time and went our separate ways.

But one more thing did happen somewhere in between the pretzel and the tower of blocks. Something so small it didn't feel worth mentioning. I had asked the happy couple how they met, more out of ritual politeness than genuine curiosity, but Maggie saw her moment. She did a swan dive into their origin story. An office encounter that really isn't worth recounting. But in the widening of her eyes and the hand gestures and the specific lilt of her voice before Sam entered the frame—the *and then* that can only lead to this man—I realized she was telling their story in a way I recognized and felt freed from. *And then and then and then*—and for myself, I don't know how to finish this sentence. For once, I am not sure of the way that it ends.

*

The largest, heaviest, most dense living organism ever found is the Pando tree, located in Utah. It looks like a forest, but it's actually a single cohesive being. It is a forest of one. Clocking in at an estimated thirteen million pounds, it encompasses over 106 acres. It has a massive underground root system, which the experts guess started at the end of the last Ice Age.

For reproduction, no seeds are necessary; new sprouts simply emerge from the roots. Every tree you see is a clone of the original. The Pando tree is genetically male. The name *Pando* comes from Latin; it means "I spread." ("That tracks," Darlene says, rolling her eyes.)

This magnificent beast is also referred to as the Trembling Giant. This nickname is so sweet to me. Goliath wearing his fear on his sleeve. If this were a fairy tale, it would be the misunderstood monster. Scientists have been monitoring the growth of its new offshoots, which have dwindled in recent years.

The oneness of the Pando tree reminds me of watching Sam tell our kids their bedtime stories; the way this scene played out in the shadows on the wall, the way his shadow always overwhelmed theirs, like they were one big being. Sam has such an easy time of seeing the kids as extensions of himself. It comes from a natural place in him that I can't seem to access in myself. Noah and Lily feel so separate from me—but not in an inherently bad way. In a way where I want to get to know them. They are their own people. Children are stories we told each other before they took on a life of their own, much like myths.

When I tell Noah about the Pando tree, he decides Utah is the dream destination for our next vacation. We plan and plan our future paths.

*

Another mother in the PTA is kicking off the meeting by sharing volunteer opportunities. These meetings are usually only held once a month, but in the flurry of back-to-school activities, the powers that be scheduled *two* for September. I let most of them wash over me—things I wouldn't be any good at or have no interest in, like community gardening and compost captaining. Everyone else is most excited about the puppy socialization with the local animal shelter. But then she says the thing that catches my ear: "The library is looking for volunteers to pick up a couple of shifts a week." They need someone to shelve books, to man the front desk, to participate in story hour—which is to say that they are looking for someone to give order to chaos, someone whose job it is to gift people the right stories at the right time. Someone to press a book into an unsuspecting patron's hands, to perform a kind of alchemy for the kids, turning the black-and-white pages into something that could light up a room.

"It's only a few hours a week," she says. Still, it's a start. On the volunteer sheet, I sign my name.

*

Lily is already excited about Halloween, even though that's weeks away. She runs around in all black and sometimes whispers/sometimes screams, "Hocus-pocus!" One day, she asks me what this means.

It comes from the Latin: *hoc est corpus meum*, or: this is my body. Self-ownership, like the tree in Georgia, is a kind of magic.

*

I have the *knock-knock* dream again. The one that goes: I'm alone in the house, and I'm in the middle of something that I have deemed important, only I can't remember what it is. When I finally pull myself away and open the door, I see that there is no one there, which is to say that the world is there at the doorstep.

*

Home Depot always smells the same. It's one of life's great comforts. That sawdust scent gives possibility a more tangible quality, lends it a body. It brings me right back to being a kid, accompanying my dad on his home improvement whims. Home Depot: the true epicenter of self-help. I find that as I get older, I'm running out of places that smell like my childhood.

My own kids run around with an excitement usually reserved for amusement parks. I think of Sam's plan to tell them about the separation at Six Flags. If only we had known we could have brought them here instead! They ogle the chandeliers, mesmerized by the rows of light. My son disappears into the gardening atrium, cupping leaves with his palms. Meanwhile my daughter pulls me toward the wall of paint swatches: the reason we're here. She's supposed to pick out a new color for her room—anything she wants, as per the self-help book's suggestion. She is absolutely transfixed by the sheer number of options before her. She can't believe this many shades exist. More colors than she has in her own toolkit. "More colors than the Crayola Sixty-Four," she whispers to me. She grabs as many swatches as she can reach, and then asks me to pick her up so she can discover the rest. "Which ones are your favorites?" I ask her. She's leaning toward the purples, I know, but she's got fistfuls of every color. She would've loved the book of hair, back in the salons of my own childhood. I imagine her stroking the boldest, most outlandish strands, like I used to do.

"What are you going to do with all these swatches?" I ask.

She shrugs. "They can be bookmarks when my books are big enough." She shuffles them like cards, like a tarot deck, before arranging them by color. She tries to sound out the words printed on each card. She has me read out the hues she doesn't recognize. She loves that there are so many names for yellow.

We reconvene with my son in the patio furniture aisle, as planned. The metal slats are cool against my skin. We slide seat cushions under my daughter. We pile them so high that she's almost eye level. My son is trying to sell me on trees. My daughter is doling out colors now, handing her brother a dark green card. "What about me?" I say, pretend hurt. "What am I? Chopped liver?"

She stares at her hands. "What color is chopped liver?" she asks slyly. She finds a brown card that actually does resemble the food and hands it over.

For weeks, she carries the swatches with her wherever she goes. She hands them out to anyone who will take one—friends, strangers we pass on the street. She does it with urgency, like she needs people to know what their true color is. I admire her decisiveness, her ability to boil down a person to the named essential.

*

One morning, I am helping my son into his backpack. I pretend it's his suit jacket and we are at a fancy restaurant. "Monsieur?" I prompt. And he goes one arm at a time.

"Do you know when the best time to plant a tree is?" he asks, with mischief balled into the corners of his eyes like sleep crusties.

He's trying to stump me, I know.

"The spring?" I ask dumbly. The obvious answer.

He tells me, "Either the spring *or* the fall. There's disagreement about it." He opens up his big tree book and points to the appropriate section: right after the ground thaws in the early spring is usually a good bet, *or* you can plant your tree in the temperate fall, to give it time to establish a root system before the draining demands of another spring/summer.

There's something beautiful about the tree-planting-season debate to me. Spring gets all the credit as the season of rebirth, but we might be kinder in giving a tree a chance to establish its support network in the quieter months. Autumn: a time for hidden growth and the subterranean layers of a person. It sounds like F. Scott Fitzgerald saying life starts over again when leaves get crisp in the fall.

"When do *you* think the best time to plant a tree here would be?" I ask him.

I am delighted when he says the fall—a subconscious affirmation that he too believes we can burrow forth into the cold and come out on the other side okay.

I tell my son we can plant a tree in the backyard. He's so excited. He spends weeks picking it out. It's all he talks about. Do we want a tree that simply flowers or one that bears fruit? I feel like a favorite again. We set a day. We make space for it. We have our hands in the dirt.

Digging takes a while when you don't have all the proper tools. My kids are trying to teach Darlene's corgi how to help us in the digging process. They get on all fours and plow their fists into the earth, showing by way of example. Roberta shows very little interest in helping and curls up elsewhere, in the shade. And then my youngest turns to me and says, "Tell me a story." She says, "The full story about you and Dad. What happened next?" I smooth her hair over with the back of my hand. "When you're older," I promise. There are some stories we grow into.

I pick up a worm with a gloved hand and offer it to my son like I think it's a gummy worm. I still find myself in a perpetual state of trying to make my kids laugh. I ask him what we should name our tree. I run through a litany of silly names: Rumpelstiltskin, John Jacob Jingleheimer Schmidt, Dog (because of the bark). But he's so focused. He stays the course. The hole gets bigger and bigger. Sometimes he reminds me of me, my son, with his hands in the dirt, still digging.

Epilogue
(or, another ending)

A few months later, I'm due for another mammogram screening. There will be more of these, I know. So many more. But if this one is clear, I won't have to come back for another six months, maybe even a year. If this one is clear, it'll feel like one less hill to roll the stone up against.

Darlene and I enter the waiting room as we have done so many times over the past several months. *This is the last time I'm going to sign in here. This is the last time I'm going to drink water from this comically small paper cup. This is the last time I'm going to put on this crinkly paper robe. (Maybe.) (For a little while.)* The way we're always writing endings.

The doctor tells me my scans look clear, and we all breathe a big sigh: a chorus of relief.

"This is great. This is really great," Darlene says in the hallway, as we wait for the famously slow elevator. "How do you feel?"

"You know it's not *over*," I say. "Not ever. Not really."

"It's still a marker of something." She hands me one of her signature Urned It™ urns. Mine is an elegant pale green, the color of shy new leaves bursting forth. When I shift it in my palms, I realize, with slight alarm, that it's not empty. "What's inside?" I ask, and she explains that she burned a few of the outdated women's magazines that we'd been stealing. These are their ashes. And . . . something else. Something else clinks around inside when I shake the vessel. She doesn't have to tell me what it is. I somehow already know: my wedding ring. "Since they wouldn't let you keep Maggie, I had to fill it with something!" she says. It's as good a place to keep it all as any. The remnants of a horrible, no good, very bad year.

Then I tell her I've forgotten something inside, that I'll be right back. I slip into the office, and I take *The Big Book of Anti-Jokes* out of my tote. I leave it there, on the table, among the sparse selection of magazines that are left. Someone will know what to do with it.

I nod to the woman in the room who is still waiting, and I shut the door behind me.

Author's Note

There are so many different versions of the myths and folktales that I've tried to evoke in this story. The ones in these pages might not be written the way you know them. I might've gotten the details wrong or left stuff out or mixed up a few characters here and there. (It is surprisingly difficult to track down certain Chinese myths!) For the most part, the myths here are written as they were told to me by my mother; in that sense, they are the truest versions I can offer you.

Acknowledgments

I am eternally grateful to Judy Clain, my brilliant editor. I still can't believe I get to work with you! Thank you for believing in this book. Thank you for your enthusiasm at every stage, for shepherding this novel into the world with such care, and for welcoming me into this fantastic family you've created at Summit. Big thanks to Josie Kals, Kevwe Okumakube, Anna Skrabacz, Laura Perciasepe, and Luiza de Campos Mello Grijns for your kindness, passion, and quick email responses to silly questions. Thank you for being the best team ever. Thanks also to Grace Han for the gorgeous cover, and to the production team whose attention to detail made the interior look so good: Paul Dippolito, Valerie Shea, Yvette Grant, and Jillian Bray. Thank you to the whole team at Simon & Schuster. You're lifesavers and life-changers, all of you.

Thank you to Duvall Osteen—a rock and a rock star. You're the best agent a girl could ask for. Thank you for spicy margaritas, for raucous dinner parties, for medical advice, for knowing that dog photos are sometimes the best thing to send. You're the perfect person to talk to when it feels like the world is ending. Thanks also to Geritza Carrasco and the entire team at UTA for patiently explaining things like foreign taxes to me.

I owe a debt of gratitude to Jessamine Chan, whose words and mentorship have meant everything. Thank you for our long phone calls, for making me feel like this was possible.

Thanks also to Madeleine Watts for her early encouragement in a Catapult workshop. (Bring it back!)

None of this would be possible without the support of the Center for Fiction, the Asian American Writers' Workshop, Kundiman, and Millay Arts. To these places and, most importantly, to the people I met there, thank you. You made this whole writing thing a lot less lonely and a lot more fun.

To the eldest daughters of PLG—Jen Lue, Gina Chung, Vanessa Chan, Kyle Lucia Wu—thank you for your wisdom and camaraderie! Drinks at the Bobbed Bandit soon?

While we're on the topic of local haunts: shout-out to the good people at Hamlet for keeping me caffeinated and to the good people at Little Mo Wine & Spirits for stocking my favorite Lambrusco.

Big love to my day ones in publishing: Kait Astrella, Dhyana Taylor, Sam Trovillion, and especially Emily Burns, who said hi to me in the Grove Atlantic kitchen when I was new; who read this work in early stages; and who held my hand throughout this entire process. A great editor and an even better friend. A thousand tiger lilies to you, Em.

A few other fine folks I want to shout out, because they've been welcoming and kind and willing to offer advice over wine or mozzarella sticks at any given time: Santilla Chingaipe, Laura Mae Pfeffer, Randy Winston, Andy Tang, Kukuwa Fraser, Natalie Green, Bret Yamanaka, August Thompson, Kevin Chau, Corinne Segal, Olivia Rutigliano, Eleni Theodoropoulos, Aaron Robertson, Jessie Gaynor, Dwyer Murphy, Dan Sheehan, and the rest of the team at Lit Hub and Grove Atlantic, where I cut my teeth.

I would be nothing and nowhere without the encouragement of my professors at Bennington. To Doug Bauer, Brooke Allen, Becky Godwin, Ben Anastas, Michael Dumanis, and Brando Skyhorse—thank you for lighting the way.

To Samantha Krause, did you know you were actually the very first reader of this story? Thank you for opening an email in 2020 (subject line: "god help me") that held the seeds of *Maggie*. Thank you for being my writing buddy.

Thank you to all my Darlenes: Samaya Abdus-Salaam, Eva Jacobs, Joseph Payne, Tatyana Aravena, Kyra Button, Rachel Sobelsohn, May Treuhaft-Ali, Jessica Yung, Basia Rosenbaum, Jorja Rose, Ash Combahee, Jeanelle Ortiz, Kam Carter, Catherine Murley, and last but certainly not least, Alex Burgess, who joked about taking my author photo when we were mere freshmen in college. I love you like a sister.

Speaking of family! Thank you to my entire family—Mom and Dad, Matthew, Eva, Irene, Chester, Chor, and Vicky—for supporting me and telling me to follow my dreams, always. Special thanks to my grandmother Lily (1936–2024). I am because of you.

To Kaleb, Aaliyah, Henry, and Beau—thanks for the jokes.

To Ollie: You probably can't read this, but thank you for keeping me company during all those late-night writing sessions. You're the best, buddy.

And, finally, a special thank-you to Andrew Unger for the dog walks and car rides and countless in-between hours spent talking about this story. For never being mad when "inspiration struck" at the exact moment when the dishes needed to be done. For being my confidant and partner in crime, always. None of this would be possible without your love, encouragement, and good humor. I am so grateful for you and for this weird little life we have built. I can't wait to continue our Home Depot vs. Lowe's debate forever. I love you so much. There. I put it in a book. No going back now!